LLOYD PETERS

---◆---

ROSE ON
THE PILLOW

Complete and Unabridged

LINFORD
Leicester

First published in Great Britain in 1983

First Linford Edition
published 2003

British Library CIP Data

Peters, Lloyd
    Rose on the pillow.—Large print ed.—
Linford romance library
1. Love stories
2. Large type books
I. Title
823.9'14 [F]

ISBN 0–7089–4981–9

Published by
F. A. Thorpe (Publishing)
Anstey, Leicestershire

Set by Words & Graphics Ltd.
Anstey, Leicestershire
Printed and bound in Great Britain by
T. J. International Ltd., Padstow, Cornwall

This book is printed on acid-free paper

ROSE ON THE PILLOW

Holidaying alone in the Algarve, Pippa Gentle finds romance with a poor, handsome fisherman. It seems like the perfect holiday, or is it? In a few days' time she must return home to her ailing mother — but her new friend has plans of his own. Pippa has to contend with jealousy, fears and doubts before attaining real happiness under the romantic skies of Portugal.

1

Pippa Gentle stood with her back to a sun warmed rock, seeing the crests arising in the blue off shore, curling ever larger then rushing to pound upon the beach in a foam of white. Irregularly shaped rocks stood out, the water still in violent motion around their bases, reflecting the restless state of her mind.

As the water drained away she sighed, echoing its sound, her eyes fixed on the largest rock, seemingly impervious and unaffected by the turbulence around. Against it her imagination formed the image of the man she had passed some few minutes ago along the beach. Was he so unaware of the feelings that he had aroused in her for him? A devil at the back of her mind mocked her. Of course he would be. How could he be anything else? She was nearing the end of the first week of her holiday and in her strolls along that particular beach had passed him several times. She smiled ruefully. He may have begun to think that for her it was the only one in Portugal.

Pippa became aware of the rock face digging into her flesh and eased herself away, glanced around her. Had she been thinking aloud? She was still alone in the tiny inlet formed by the curving of the low cliffs — their rocky outcrops at each side making it private for a while until other people came along. Behind her, just above the green top of the cliff, she could see the unfinished apartments, scaffolded and empty to the breeze. Two storied, not too obtrusive, and matching those set either side of the road up from the main beach.

Perhaps next year when they were finished and occupied that tiny inlet where she stood would be private no more. But just for now it was all hers, a perfect heaven or would be if — She glanced at the outcrop beyond which stretched the larger beach.

She sat down on the sand, hunched over her knees, staring ahead. The whole thing was stupid. She had been enjoying her late holiday until three days ago, when he had nodded and smiled quietly in response to her polite greeting as she had strolled along the beach one morning. It had been like a physical strike upon her somewhere between the breasts and the pit of her stomach. In a second all preconceived notions of the man she would fall in love with vanished. In that time she knew, and had walked on, her thoughts in a turmoil, to the place where she was now sat. Now a deep and hopeless ache overlay the former delight in her holiday.

She rose to her feet, undecided what to do next and half hoping that when she retraced her steps he would not be there. She must throw the feeling off. If not her holiday would be spoiled, and she might as well go home. She didn't even know his name and had had no conversation with him. One week left. How on earth was she going to make him feel toward her the way she felt towards him? What could she hope to accomplish in that time? She took a deep breath and prepared to go back. Perhaps a bus ride that afternoon away from the beach. In fact she would keep away from that particular one from now on. There were plenty more and many places to visit.

Pippa paused, looked down at herself, at her low cut bikini costume in light blue and white. Tugged a matching half sleeved jacket from her beach bag and threw it on. The sun was hot and she was fair of skin. Besides she'd heard that foreign women that were too uncovered were frowned upon locally. A few male heads had turned already that morning she had noticed. That had given her a faint pleasure, but the aching remained.

She splashed her way slowly round on to the main beach. He was still there, bending over a boat drawn up with others upon the shore. The cooling breeze played on her and was pleasant after the hot confines of the inlet. She glanced up toward the terrace with its tables and umbrellas, and behind it the gently waving palms and pines against the pure blue. Should she go up there now and have a drink? It was, she guessed, about eleven o'clock and getting busy. Her eyes strayed again to the figure by the boat. No, she would walk along the edge of the surf to where the cliff path began to the next village of Allemura. Then she would return along the top of the beach to the terrace.

The voice mocked her again loud against the water. The walk was of no interest, she only wanted to pass him again with the chance that she might speak to him. Oh, why had she to see him in the first place! She had been content in a way, resigned at twenty-three to whatever life as a spinster lay ahead for her. Now romance — a one-sided romance — held her cruelly.

As she drew nearer she saw that he was painting the boat and facing her way over its curving high prow. Concentrating, she thought, like a lover as he stroked the brush upon it. The side towards her glistened in the sun, blue, white and green. She was about ten yards away and would soon be abreast of him. Had he seen her? Did he care? Her feet left the water to walk along its edge. Perhaps he cared more about his boat than about any woman.

At that moment he stepped back, eyeing his work from stem to stern. Gave a little nod of satisfaction, then glanced sideways at Pippa. She caught the glance, hesitated. He was aware of her. She turned, took a step towards him. 'Good morning.' She had already nodded to him that day, but this gave her the opportunity to open some sort of conversation. He gave a little nod of the head in her direction, then turned and dipped his brush again.

It was now or never, she thought. Was

she being a stupid fool? What did it matter? Another week and the holiday would be just a few photographs.

'It's very beautiful.' The colours were — she knew little about boats, but it had a graceful, high, curving line to it. She saw a twitch of his mouth as the brush moved to and fro, the strokes of light blue upon its upper part. She felt like a young child staring, but without the innocence.

He straightened, a frown on his face. Spoke at the boat, 'Not good. I paint too much in sun.' Gave a little shrug, then looked at her for a moment, then back to the craft.

Pippa moved nearer. 'But the other side looks very pretty,' she said encouragingly. They had spoken together at last and in English.

He gestured toward the other side. 'I do that at sunset — better,' he said with a slight movement of pot and brush.

Her heart was beating faster. At least they were talking, even though it involved the technicalities of boat painting. The smell of hot wood and paint came to her, and she hoped that nobody else would come along just then.

He stood gazing at his handiwork with a serious intensity and she observed his dark lean profile and the slightly hooked nose. A flat dark grey cap was tilted over his eyes, its rear edge sitting on a ridge in the bush of dark hair projecting from beneath it, making it appear too small. He had on a roll neck brown jersey with another vee-necked grey one on top. Shapeless trousers were tucked into fisherman's boots. He seemed quite tall, perhaps because she herself was barefoot. He must be boiled with all those clothes on, she thought, though she had noticed that all the fishermen were dressed heavily. It made her feel quite naked standing there, in spite of the top she had put on. Was he married or engaged? What else could she say? Could always fall back on the weather.

She brushed her hair away from her face.

'You are English?' he said surveying his work.

'Yes.' She was pleased, very pleased that he had spoken and it was up to her now to keep the conversation going. But there seemed nothing to add.

'I tell the English by the teapots.' He nodded at the terrace, then glanced round at her and she saw the gleam of humour in his eyes. So dark as to be almost black and narrowed against the sun.

She smiled. 'I'm afraid we do drink a lot of it, even in hot places. Drinking hot tea is supposed to be refreshing and cooling, but I've often thought that rather odd.'

He dripped his brush and commenced his strokes again, and Pippa wondered how long it would be before she could think of something else to say, and reflected on how English she sounded, even to herself. She looked away, wondering whether she should leave it at that and walk on and not show her eagerness to stay.

Cries and screams of laughter came from the water's edge as the few intrepid bathers collapsed under the oncoming breakers. Elsewhere, a few strolled along the shore line and others lay sunbathing. Apart from the busy terrace, it was a quiet scene.

His voice came again. He was looking at her. Turned away when their eyes met. He addressed his boat. 'You not feel cold?'

'No, this is warmer than our summer is usually. This is summer time to me.' At least, she thought, he was noticing things about her, even if it was her clothing, or lack of it.

He prodded at his jersey with his brush handle. 'Winter to me — November . . . ' Wriggled his shoulders in a movement of distaste.

If this was November, thought Pippa, then let it be November the year round. The colours, the warm wind, the holiday. Oranges hanging from the

10

branches. And back home, the dead leaves of autumn would be thick, the stone walls dripping wet. The lowering shades of grey, the heavy clouds awaiting their chance, and the early black nights. The drabness of mind that it brought to a person living in the shadow of the dark hills.

A fawn coloured dog ambled up and squatted between them in friendly fashion, looked up at her inquiringly. So many dogs, ownerless it seemed. She'd noticed them before. They looked well enough though. She reached into the pocket of her jacket, felt the soft remains of some chocolate. Gave it to the dog which chewed it once then swallowed it with a gulping motion and looked for more.

The fisherman made a movement with his boot at the dog, whereupon it loped off along the beach. He glanced at her. 'Dog shake sand, water, hair. Go on paint,' he explained.

'Oh, I'm sorry, I didn't think. I feel sorry for the dogs.' She was forgetting, not all foreigners liked them.

He spread the brush and paint pot apart, mouth corners lengthening, taking any reproof away. 'All right, but paint and dogs not good together.' Their looks met, and for a moment she lost herself in the dark face opposite. 'Is this your boat?' she asked, glancing away with an effort.

'I share it to fish.' Then he looked beyond her, pointed with his brush. 'Priaia de Allemura — Allemura beach. I have other one — my own.' She saw the pride spring suddenly into his face. 'I helped to build it.' Again his pot and brush measured the air, 'Not big — just . . . ' His shoulders moved and the pride lingered.

She wondered why he needed another. 'Do you fish with that also?'

He shook his head slowly, firmly. A tolerant smile played about his lips. The question seemed to amuse him. 'Some day I sail away.'

Pippa gazed at him in some surprise. Almost everyone she knew wanted to escape from something. But why him? From what appeared to be such an idyllic place, or so it seemed to her. It was impossible that anybody should want to leave. Maybe he did not earn much, but other things counted: The climate, the tranquillity, the slower pace of life there. She herself was a typist at a large building society, on an average wage which did not by any means qualify her as rich — not financially. Rich in health, yes, able to come abroad on holiday. Yes, for sure she was rich, in that sense.

He had stopped painting, was observing her out of the corners of his eyes. What to say next! She felt awkward. 'You speak good English.'

'Many English come here. I like English. I talk with them. I learn to speak it.' He resumed his painting.

She wondered how many more girls had thought he was the one for them. Of course he liked the English. He was hardly likely to say otherwise. He would say the same thing to women of other nationalities, no doubt. Her spirits dropped suddenly. She would move on — she was only making things worse for herself — would walk to the end of the beach and back, and up to the terrace for a coffee. She became aware that he was regarding her again.

'You are thinking, always you are thinking. I see you each morning here.'

A warmth came to her face, not all from the sun. So he had noticed her. Oh, if only she could let go, tell him there and then, risk the indignity of a refusal of her advances. Why had life to be so devious? If only he could know her thoughts. Perhaps he did. 'It's so beautiful here.' Empty words. Not what she wanted to say at all.

He nodded. 'Have you long time for holiday?'

'The remainder of this week. I return on Saturday,' she said flatly with a sigh. It wasn't a fraction of the time she needed.

'Other time, eh?' He looked at her from under his cap's peak, his teeth showing slightly with his slow smile. 'I look for you, eh?'

She made herself return it brightly. 'Yes, you'll see me walking the beach again every morning.'

Oh, why couldn't he look for her now? The real her, now. There would never be another time. You couldn't plan ahead like that — things happened.

'D'you live nearby?' she asked. He jerked his head in a vague direction away from the beach, uttered something which she didn't catch. It didn't matter. 'I live in the North of England,' she volunteered. 'It'll be raining, no doubt.'

He glanced around at her. 'Better you live here, eh?' There was a provocative gleam in his eyes.

'Wish I could,' she agreed. And married to you, she thought fervently.

There was a silence between them. Pippa knew she ought to go — leave him. She didn't want him to think she was searching for a man — any man. More people were coming down on to the beach now, while others lay glistening, half in the shade of their umbrellas.

'What is your name?' His voice and its question sent a quiver of pleasure and hope through her. 'So I know the next time you come,' he added.

'Pippa.'

'Peepa?' His brow wrinkled.

She smiled at his pronunciation. 'Yes, I was christened Phillipa, but as a child I couldn't say it properly, and it came out as Pippa, and it's been Pippa ever since.'

'Phillipa, yes, good name. Portuguese. We have Filipa.'

'And what is your name?' She tried to keep her voice light and easy.

He made a gesture combining face, shoulders, pot and brush. 'Tomas. Very . . . ' he was searching for a word, 'ordinary. Not like Peepa.' His smile widened.

Pippa's heart was beginning to thump. They had only exchanged names — yet it was a beginning, and he

16

had asked for hers first. But then the ache in her heart increased. Prolonging the conversation would only make matters worse.

She forced herself to begin to move away. 'I'm just going to finish my walk on here and then it'll be time for coffee or something. Hope your boat and paint are all right.

'You be here tomorrow — you see,' he called after her, then resumed his painting. But if Pippa had glanced back a few moments later she would have seen his attention directed not upon the boat but after her.

Later, she sat at the back of the terrace sipping slowly at a large tonic and small gin: amongst the shading crumpled hats, the glitter of tea pots, the tinkle of glasses and ice, the hum of voices and overall the smell of food from the restaurant behind.

From where she was, she could just see the surf breaking on the shore and the prows of the fishing boats drawn up along the upper beach. She could see

17

nothing of Tomas or his boat. It was just as well, she reflected. But even so her mind was restless, eager to catch and hold on to anything he had said — magnify it and read into it more than was there. Had he not said for her to see the results of his handiwork tomorrow? Part of her mind dismissed it. He was just being polite. She had shown interest so it was natural he should say that. No doubt he was talking to another lightly clad female already.

Pippa put on her sunglasses against the glare, still busy with her thoughts. Something brushed her leg. She looked down; a fawn coloured Labrador sat looking up at her, panting slightly in the heat. One of the strays again. She noticed that it had no right front foot. It looked well fed as most of them did that frequented the terrace and beach. She had noticed others that were lame or scarred. Knocked down by cars perhaps?

She fell to thinking about that

afternoon and decided to keep away from the beach and take a bus ride to a new shopping complex and marina along the coast. Presents to take home with her would keep her mind off the man on the beach. Nevertheless as she left the terrace, her eyes strayed to his figure still bending over his boat.

That evening in her hotel Pippa felt restless and unable to settle in one place for long. She dined in the restaurant then sat for a while in the tasteful blue and silver lounge, listening to the pianist. She had coffee and tried to relax in the deep soft comfort of the low settees under the Moorish architecture.

The music and atmosphere was romantic, and groups and couples sat close together talking intently, laughing, happy. Where was her romance? A circle of men, jovial, sat nearby, glasses of beer in their hands, red faced from walking the golfing greens. She'd seen them earlier that day with their bags setting out for one of the nearby courses; had noticed their glances in her direction. Without their wives?

She finished her coffee and went to her room, stood looking out over the balcony. It was dark though still early. The pool lay undisturbed immediately below, empty sunbeds still in rows by its side. Beyond it two ribbons of light showed the road running straight to the beach. Brightly lit buildings alternated with gaps of darkness. No doubt, she thought, those dark areas would soon go as new building progressed. It would be a pity.

To her right, the town of Allemura lay sparkling and coloured in the night. Pippa's eyes returned to the far end of the road. A row of white lights lay spread out in the darkness below the horizon. The fishing fleet. Was he — Tomas — out there? She cupped her face in her hands and leaned heavily on the cool balcony top. She must face facts. It was just a holiday romance — not even that really. Something to be forgotten as soon as the plane was airborne in a few days' time.

The sound of music from the other bar in the hotel floated upwards. What was she doing moping in her bedroom, and it not yet ten o'clock? She should be enjoying herself, making the most of her remaining time on holiday. In another few days she would be shivering at the approach of another northern winter.

Going home brought thoughts of her mother with whom she lived. Two heart attacks had made her a semi invalid. Pippa's father had died suddenly after a severe stroke, and she was sure that the shock of his death had induced her mother's first attack. She remembered her own reaction to his passing five years before. The savage, inconceivable dagger strike to her innermost being. Now she helped her mother — tried to make life as comfortable as possible. Her brother, John, some few years older, was married with children, and lived in the south, so the burden — such as it was — fell on herself.

A taxi horn below startled her out of her thoughts, and she turned and stepped between the curtained glass doors into the bedroom. Got undressed, ready for bed, her clothes falling where they would, she stared critically at the naked reflection in the full length mirror, miserable, and angry with herself for being so. Vivid blue eyes in the framework of tumbled fair hair stared back at her, noted the medium height, slimmish and straight, curving buttocks. Too big? The same could be said of her thighs. Breasts not bad, but not as pronounced as she would have liked. She certainly looked English enough. Good teeth. She summoned a wry smile. Like a horse! Certainly she could do with some patting and petting.

In her imagination she saw Tomas appear behind her through the mirror, his arms enfold her, his hands strong, yet fine, hairy, caressing her. His words of love. But his image soon began to wane. Naked she was, and going to bed on holiday at ten o'clock. Friends had accused her of being too choosy — of missing the marriage boat. She had had a few men friends, but none had reached her heart, and even a proposal of marriage from one at work. But she had waited. Now she had found the man and to no avail. She glanced towards the balcony. If he was not fishing, was he lying with another woman, his toes in the sand?

She turned away from the mirror, depressed by the thought. Got into bed, determined that she would not on any account visit that beach again. Being a fool to herself, and spoiling her holiday. She drew a mental line at the top of the road leading to the beach. The line which was to signify the end of one chapter in her life, and the beginning of a new one.

2

The next morning she awakened to the familiar pop popping sound of motor scooters coming up the main road bringing their riders to work at the unfinished building near the hotel. Pippa wandered on to the balcony. The sun was just beginning to yellow and warm it. She never ceased to be amazed at the certainty and the regularity with which its rays touched then covered the wall dividing her balcony from the next. All looked well for another lovely day.

One hour after breakfast found her on the beach. Her will power and determinations of the night before crumbling a quarter mile from the hotel. At the cross roads she had meant to turn right, wait for a bus to Allemura. For some reason her sandals had taken her feet straight ahead, continuing past the outdoor chairs and coffee drinkers, past the apartments and then down the hill. She knew she was like a gambler — just once more, and ashamed at her own weakness.

There was no sign of Tomas, his boat standing resplendent in its new colours without him. She tried to think of it as a fortunate occurrence, and struck out across the beach. It was already hot and she decided to bathe. The water felt cold and she waded in gradually, but then a huge breaker rolled in and caught her, knocking her down and carrying her inshore along with it. Once immersed she returned time and time again into the approaching surf, flinging herself into its white foam. It was as if she was deliberately trying to wash all memories away under the shock of the cold sea, exaggerating her movements in a subconscious effort to break free from the web of emotion with which she had surrounded herself.

Afterwards, and tired with her exertions, she sat in the shade of a rock, her back against its warmth, and relaxed, trying to keep her mind empty of anything to do with the owner of the boat along the beach. She must have dozed off, for when she opened her eyes, the sun was hot on her and a few holiday makers had settled nearby. She looked in her bag for her watch. After twelve! Brushing the sand from herself, she threw her sun top on to protect her shoulders. An iced pineapple and vodka with a coffee afterwards would be perfect, then perhaps a walk along the path below the cliffs to Allemura. She felt refreshed, determined and more stable.

Standing up, bag over shoulder, hat in hand, she glanced over the rock towards the terrace. A figure was busy at the stern of Tomas's boat. She couldn't make out whether it was him or not. She put on her sun glasses and the big floppy white hat above them, then took a deep breath and strode purposefully towards the steps ascending to the terrace. These were about twenty-five yards from the first of the line of fishing boats drawn up on the shore. That way she would not have to pass Tomas, if indeed it were him.

This was the testing time, she told herself. This was the battle with herself that she must win. Even so, she was aware that it was Tomas as she drew near. Pulling her hat well down she grasped the wooden rail. Nine steps and he would be a memory. Round the side of the kiosk at the top and she would be free. Never to return to that beach.

The third step.

'Hey, Pippa.'

The voice made her jump visibly. She turned, acting her surprise, but her heart was already giving the lie to her previous intentions. Rested her foot on the next step.

'Miss English.'

She saw his face above the boats. Moved downwards one step. How had he recognised her? Anyway, she had tried.

He made a small private waving

motion of his hand towards himself.

Her feet touched the sand. She hadn't really wanted to leave it without meeting him again. She knew the truth. It was fate. A musical she remembered — Kismet — fate. Walked slowly, still acting, but pulled towards him as if on the end of a rope which the fishermen used to haul the boats ashore.

'I look for you. I think you are not walking this morning.'

'I was down earlier than usual.' She saw that he had been washing his outboard engine and its cover.

He rested his arm on the casing, the water from the sponge in his hand dribbling down its white metal. 'I see you in water.' Shook his head briefly at the mad women of England. 'In and out, very brave, cold.' An admiring smile played round his mouth.

'I was hot, it was very refreshing.' If only he knew why she had attacked the sea so vigorously.

He lifted a hand at the boat. 'All right

now, eh?' The dark eyes enslaved her again.

'Yes, it's beautiful.' It was. 'I noticed it earlier.'

He tapped the engine casing with the hand holding the sponge. 'Salt water no good for metal. I clean it off.'

Pippa nodded in understanding.

He began to swill the water over it again from the plastic bucket, and she noticed that he was barefoot, trousers rolled up to hairy calves. Say goodbye now, an urgent voice inside her cried. Why torture herself further? Just because he had looked for her did not mean anything.

He glanced up to meet her gaze. 'You like boats, eh?'

She wrinkled her nose. 'Not when it's rough and not if they're noisy.' Waved her hand at the calm water offshore. 'But on a day like today I prefer sailing boats.' Her companion nodded. Her answer seemed to please him. Actually she liked the big liners, though she'd only been on a short cruise once

— they always seemed so romantic. Air travel did not seem so. And sailing boats always seemed elegant, graceful and peaceful.

She noticed that he had a gold coloured ring on the fourth finger of his right hand with a fancy design of two circles engraved upon a black background.

'Are you with friend?' He dropped the sponge into the bucket.

She shook her head. 'I'm alone — on holiday by myself.'

He rubbed his hands on his trousers, gave a little shrug and the mouth widened. 'You think I ask questions, but if you not busy tonight, mebbe you come and watch putting boat out for fishing.'

Pippa's heart took off again. Her pleasure must have been very evident to him. 'I'd be glad to — thank you very much. I've seen the lights from my balcony at night. What time will you be . . . ?'

Tomas screwed up his face. 'Mebbe

30

eight — about.' He bent and took a cloth from the bucket, wrung it out and started to wipe the engine casing.

She began to turn away. Didn't mind going now. She was to meet him again. Her heart was full, but her mind cautioned that she must not read too much into it. It was, after all, only to watch the boats go out. 'Until tonight, goodbye,' she called over her shoulder.

'Bom dia, Pippa.'

She ascended the steps, lightly, easily. The coffee and her vodka on the terrace tasted far better than they would have done an hour before. Afterwards she went for a walk taking the cliff path to where it joined the platform of flat rocks beside the sea. The sun was high and hot, and she felt its heat reflected from the reddish face of the cliffs close by.

Once she sat down and watched the sea breaking foaming white against the rocks further out, then come rushing inwards to thrust upwards through holes in the rocks, to burst in a fountain of spray nearby. It was cooling and hypnotic as it spattered her face and dried almost immediately. Tomas was the sea, and she the rocks, waiting. Pippa dreamed, then afterwards continued her walk, a voice inside her repeating, fool! fool!

Shortly after eight o'clock that evening found her, with a few other spectators, looking out over the beach from the terrace. The moon was nearly full, silvering the sea, and silhouetting figures near it and those boats already out. She recognised Tomas's boat down on the beach and saw two men by it. It was difficult to see whether he was one of them. The boat was halfway to the water. One of the figures was placing something on the ground ahead of the craft. He then came towards the stern. As he did so she saw the blur of his face turned to the terrace. Saw his hand wave. And again. Must be Tomas. Did he want her to go down? She hesitated, then heard her name as only he could pronounce it.

As she approached, he said something to his companion, then hailed her. "Allo, boa noite — good night Pippa. I think you not coming.'

Would he have cared if she had not? she wondered, pulling her cardigan more closely around her.

'Cold?' he enquired.

'No, not really, it's a lovely evening.'

He gave a little shrug. 'We put boat in,' he stated simply, and with that he and his friend pushed hard on the stern, their bodies like props against it. Pippa saw that it was resting on strips of wood and as the boat moved forward over them, it left some behind. Tomas then picked these up and then placed them in front of the boat, the process being repeated until it reached the sea. She walked alongside feeling rather neglected and helpless, and when she saw them both pushing again she placed a tentative hand alongside Tomas's as a token gesture of help. The boat slid some yards, then stopped and Tomas looked up. 'Your help good.' She saw the amusement on both faces.

Suddenly she felt foolish, uncomfortable. She shouldn't have come down on to the beach. To watch would have been sufficient.

Tomas must have caught something of her feeling. 'Your hands get dirty, beautiful clothes spoiled.' His manner was gentle. 'Not woman's work.' He picked up the strips of wood, placed them in front of the boat, then came back. 'I ask you to come on the beach, but not to work, huh?' For the first time she saw him smile broadly, his teeth gleaming in the moonlight.

A few minutes later they had progressed to the water's edge. Another push and the prow began to move to the waves. Pippa stood back watching, wishing that she was barefoot and could have gone further. But then she saw Tomas leave his companion holding the side of the boat and come towards her. He stopped in front of her, his face in deep shadow.

'You like to see my other boat

sometime, Pippa? With sails?'

Her heart lifted at once. 'Oh, yes I would.' She waited eagerly.

'I not here in morning. You meet me at crossroads — near your hotel. At bus stop, dois.'

She must have looked blank. Glimpsed his smile. 'Desculpe — sorry — two — at two.' For a moment he hesitated and she knew that he was looking straight at her though she could not see his expression. Then he turned away. 'Tomorrow. Boa noite, Pippa.'

'Tomorrow,' she called after him. 'Goodnight Tomas.' It felt good to say his name — a bond between them.

She remained where she was and watched as Tomas and his friend pushed once more. Then his companion clambered quickly into the boat and started to row hard. A few yards out and Tomas joined him, but standing at the stern. The boat reared under the first large wave, its prow pointing towards the sky, but then came down just when Pippa thought it would overturn. Suddenly the engine fired noisily and the boat gathered way and the rower stopped.

Pippa saw the light at the stern come on. Thought she saw the movement of an arm, and waved back and remained waving occasionally until the boat and occupants had blended with the sea, and its light was a pinprick in the darkness.

★ ★ ★

At two o'clock the next day Pippa stood on the board walk under an awning outside a shop near the bus stop at the crossroads. It was dusty and hot. She wondered if she was standing on the right side of the road to meet Tomas. She had forgotten to ask from which direction he would approach. Cars and taxis went by and the occasional bus, one stopping near her, its sunblinds down and on the way to Allemura.

She gazed across the road at the new buildings under construction, then glanced at her watch. Doubt began to creep into her mind. Was he not going to meet her? Was she going to be stood up? Perhaps already, he and his friend were sitting in a bar somewhere having a good laugh at her expense. Another five minutes and she would take the next bus, no matter in which direction it was going. She blinked against the glare, not wearing her sunglasses, in case he did not recognise her with them on. The brightness of mind and excitement which had built up in her that morning was beginning to leave her. She had been unable to settle to anything, sitting round the hotel pool and avoiding looking at the notice board with its reminder of the day of departure.

A horn sounded to her left. A black and green taxi stood a few yards away. An arm beckoned to her from its window. He had come. She hurried over to the passenger side, the door already open for her. Glanced in. There was no Tomas. Only the driver, an older man wearing a yellow panama hat. She drew back in her disappointment, but he motioned at the seat.

'Miss Pippa Gentle? I take you to Allemura.'

He bent forward, took a note from the dash, handed it to her. 'Tomas — telephone.'

She looked at the address, *33, Apartamentos, Calleres*. He must have seen the doubt on her face, for he smiled with a pleasant indifference, 's'all right, I take you to Apartamentos Calleres.'

She got in somewhat apprehensive, but glad that Tomas had not let her down after all. She was puzzled though. Why had he not come to meet her as arranged?

They set off in the direction of Allemura, Pippa comforting herself with the thought that it was broad daylight, and the town only a few minutes away. But Tomas had mentioned showing her his sailing boat. Perhaps they were going to eat first.

There was nothing to worry about, she told herself. She was after all going to meet him again — the man who had for most of her holiday occupied her waking thoughts. Boat or Allemura, it made no difference. It was Tomas who mattered to her.

They passed what Pippa called the Pottery tree — she'd seen it before. A tree by the road side with objects made of pot hanging from its branches. Cups, urns, plates caught the eye. A good advertisement and no doubt brought a lot of business. The small workshop was just behind it. She was reminded that she must buy some presents soon. Perhaps that afternoon if she and Tomas went into Allemura itself.

She looked down at herself, wondered if she were overdressed in that heat. In a white buttoned down the middle towelling dress, but bare-armed.

Soon they were in the town — in the narrow streets squeezing the car between the buses and the house walls, avoiding the pedestrians. The diesel and petrol fumes, and the political pamphlets stuck to the shuttered windows, served to spoil the entry into the town.

They rounded into the main square with its market stalls, trees, and small park with its fountain. She glimpsed a barrow, a stove atop it with its long pipe. Roasted chestnuts. How she'd enjoyed them a few days ago. A handful wrapped in old telephone pages. Pippa smiled to herself. How strange to find hot chestnuts being sold in such a sunny warm climate.

She became aware that the car was climbing up and away from the square, between white houses and apartments hugging the steep hillside. The road twisted and turned and Pippa glimpsed courtyards, shady alcoves, and narrow alleyways. The ground levelled off and the car stopped. The driver motioned her to get out. She saw that they were outside a block of apartments, glaring white, with balconies, and pine trees behind them. It was hot, with a slight breeze, and very quiet. No one was about. Below, the town and the flat blue of the sea. She thought it was like being partially deaf — the sound was there but muted.

The man beckoned her to follow him through an archway dividing the apartments. They looked new, empty, no one on the balconies. Thoughts flashed through Pippa's mind. Did Tomas live here? They looked more like holiday homes than a fisherman's. And why meet her here? The shade beneath the archway was pleasant, then briefly into the sunshine again, and her guide pointing at an open door at the rear of the apartments. Steps led upwards.

He stopped, waited and she came abreast of him. Why was Tomas not there to greet her?

Apprehension returned, the stairway seemed dark, made more so after the brightness outside. She looked at the man who had brought her. Saw the quick smile and nod upwards, then he walked away and left her. It was not what she had expected.

41

She mounted one flight slowly. A landing and a door. She guessed that would be to the first floor apartment. Another flight and the door of Thirty-three she found was open halfway. Excitement returned at the prospect of seeing Tomas again. She pushed the door wider, and stepped inside. 'Tomas,' she called. There was no answer.

The hall was lit by electric light, so was the room beyond. Perhaps he was in there. She went forward into it. 'Tomas — it's Pippa.' The room was empty, silent. There was no one. She stood there perplexed and disappointed. It was the right apartment — Number Thirty-three. The door had been open as if she had been expected. But where was Tomas? Had he just stepped out for a moment or had the taxi driver made a mistake, getting the right number, but the wrong block of apartments?

The dull thud of the outer door closing came from behind. Startled, then pleased that it must be Tomas returning, she hurried into the hall to greet him. But there was no Tomas. Just herself standing alone in front of the closed door. She tried to open it. It had no handle on the inside. Called out. It was no good.

Back in the room a vertical chink of light showed where the balcony window would be, but heavy wooden shutters covered this from floor to ceiling, and where the usual sliding glass door on to the balcony should have been was another solid one. Bending down she put her eye to the crack. A strip of blue on white — sky and balcony wall.

She sank down on to the settee glad of the electric light in the low ceiling. It would be dark and oppressive without it. Confused by the events of the last half hour she struggled to get some sort of order into her thoughts. It was difficult.

What had happened to Tomas? The call purporting to come from him had got her there.

She became aware of the sheet of paper with writing on it on the low table in front of her. She picked it up. The words big and black hit her eyes. 'We mean no harm to you. Do not be frightened. You will be kept here for a short time. There is food, bed, and blankets.'

She'd wake up on the beach soon. This was a bad dream — it must be. But she knew it wasn't. Wind had not shut the door, there was none. Someone had come up after her and closed it.

The knowledge of what it might be gnawed at her incredulous mind. A kidnapping attempt? Her thoughts stumbled about. Why would anyone kidnap her? Why was anyone kidnapped? For money. But she had none, not enough to make it worthwhile to anyone. And yet . . . Pippa made an effort to calm herself, to assemble her thoughts. Perhaps Tomas had spoken about their meeting. Had been overheard and she was imprisoned here as a result. And she herself had been very foolish taking it for granted that he had sent the message and the taxi. But he was not the sort of man who would open his mouth to everyone about anything, she was sure of that, even though she had only known him for a short time. Now she would probably never see him again.

Head in her hands, she slumped. Pippa Gentle, ordinary typist, kidnapped. And outside the suburbs slumbered on, white and dazzling.

3

Later she moved about the room restlessly. How long were her captors prepared to keep her there? And how long before the hotel people realised that she was missing? A flash of hope rose in her at this latter. She was due out on Saturday, it was now Tuesday. They would look for her when she had not settled her account. Go to her room. See her clothes and other things still there. They would search for her. Perhaps Tomas, when she was reported missing, would lead the search for her. Amongst his own people he may hear something.

She went to the outer door, put her mouth to the lock. Shouted for help until she was hoarse. Then did the same at the crack in the wooden shutters, but to no avail. Nothing happened. She looked for other means of escape but found none. To one side of the hall were a kitchen and a bathroom and toilet, and across was the bedroom. Again all the windows were shuttered.

Pippa searched for something with which to try and prise at the wood, but plastic knives and some crockery were all she found. She comforted herself with the thought that if she could convince them that she was not rich and offered them all the money she had with her, then perhaps they would allow her to leave. She would promise not to say anything about the affair. Suddenly, she wanted to be back home in Halford again, in the drizzle, treading on leaves brought down by autumn-like winds before summer had begun. Away from the hard glare outside, that electric light inside, and the place which had now made her fearful.

In the kitchen she found a bowl of salad and rice, a dish of fresh fruit and bread. A plastic bottle of orange juice stood nearby. On a plate were piled wrapped squares of butter like those she had had in her hotel. Her captors certainly did not intend her to go hungry, or suffer hardship. But she had very little appetite, and just made herself a salad sandwich and drank of the orange juice.

The hours passed. Once she crept to the outer door, stood silent and listening intently, heard nothing. Was there someone on guard outside the door? She was beginning to think that perhaps there was only one man involved in the affair. If that were true, she may have a better chance of escaping.

Pippa put her eye to the crack between the shutters. Purple had replaced the daylight. Night had come. Twilight was shorter in the southern latitude, she remembered. Not the slow, reluctant approach of evening after an English summer's day. She began to feel cool. Found a blanket in the bedroom, draped it around her shoulders. She had no other clothing with her but the light dress she wore.

She sat huddled on the settee wishing she could make a cup of tea. It had become a habit with her at home, a cup last thing at night before bed. One for her mother also. At the hotel they made weak stuff from tea bags. Even that would have been nice now.

Pippa decided she was not going to sleep — dare not. Would stay where she was, dressed. She wondered what Tomas had thought when she had not been there to meet him. Surely he would have thought it strange. She was sorry, very sorry. She had been close to love. Had been in love in fact. Now it would be over. Her brief exciting flirtation with the shadow of love was past. It had been one-sided anyway, and certainly there was no chance now of it being anything else. Not unless she was freed before Saturday. If that happened she would dash straight to the beach. Show herself to him, hope to see the surprise and delight in his dark eyes. Fisherman he may be now, but two or three centuries before in lighter colourful clothes, barefoot on the prow of a larger boat, sword in hand, challenging gleaming eyes searching the nearing shore for plunder. If only he could come to her aid now, athletically climbing up the balcony, thrusting the shutters aside. She dozed off into fitful sleep.

She awoke with stiffened limbs just after eight o'clock to hear the faint barking of a dog somewhere. For a moment she was undecided as to where she was. Memories slid back presenting all the earlier anxieties. Nevertheless, woman-like her attention was taken by her dress, creased and crumpled from lying on it, and a few minutes later at the sight of her haggard face and unbrushed hair in the bathroom mirror. After washing and improving her appearance as best she could she breakfasted on orange juice and an apple sandwich. Tired humour told her it would be good for her figure if nothing else. Then she sat down again and tried to compose herself to await whatever the rest of the day may bring. She must be brave.

An hour later she heard the main door being opened. She stood up, her heart suddenly increasing its beat. Braced herself. She was English — try to keep her dignity. A Yorkshire girl, and grit was one of the features of the Yorkshire character. For a wild moment she thought of rushing into the passage. Snatching at a chance whilst the door was open. A swift chopping of the hand upon the opponent, and down they dropped — on television anyway. But it wasn't like that in real life.

The sound of the door closing stopped any further thoughts on that particular aspect of escape. A few moments later a figure in white appeared in the doorway facing her, a cowled hood pulled so far over the head as to make it seem a dark empty cavity. From the shoulders down hung a voluminous nightshirt type of garment. It reminded her of figures on postcards from North Africa. Bare feet in sandals

51

poked from beneath the hem.

Pippa stayed where she was. Tried to firm her voice. 'What do you want?' It was a silly question, she was aware. They were after money, but the act of speaking relaxed the tension somewhat in her.

'Look,' she went on desperately, 'I haven't got much money, I'm just not rich. You've got the wrong person.' She suddenly realised she might be talking to no avail. The figure may not understand English, even though the note was written in it. 'Do you understand me?'

The figure nodded.

'You understand English?'

Another nod.

'Well, let me go then. You're wasting your time and my holiday. D'you realise that I only get three weeks a year? If I had the money you could have it, though it wouldn't do you any good.' Her voice was sounding harsh, she knew. She was tired, her nerves taut now. Before, she had not wanted to show her anger, thinking that it would impede her release. If only Tomas would walk in through that door. Take her on the afternoon's outing as they had planned.

'You had no right to bring me here, keep me here,' she continued angrily. 'I made a date to meet Tomas. I kept that date. Now he will think I didn't care.' Great anxiety filled her suddenly. 'He's all right, isn't he? You haven't harmed him?' Pippa tried to penetrate the gloom beneath the hood in front of her.

She saw the shake of it, felt relief but some anxiety remained. They would only tell her what they wanted her to know. Then to her surprise the figure stepped forward to pick up the pen and paper from the table. He wrote something then passed the pad to her.

Pippa read it. '*You like Tomas?*' it asked. She stared over it at the writer, her feelings quickly and plainly on her face. Like Tomas! Much, much more than that. A shooting star had risen in the heavens, touched earth, borne her along on an arching fireway of love, then returned her cruelly, too soon. She would never feel its like again.

She returned the pad to the waiting hand, the figure moved back to the doorway and wrote again. Tore a page out, gave it to her. On it was written, 'Tomas *like you. Call you English rose,*' She felt her cheeks warming. He had liked her! He must have told them. By the sound of things he had said a lot about her. Yet again she felt that he was not the sort of man to talk about his private affairs. And yet, it appeared that he had. English rose! She had obviously had more effect on him than she had realised. But too late now. The rose was feeling battered, dejected, and drooping.

Pippa stood with the sheet of paper in her hands, read the words again. Somehow they gave her encouragement. He had liked her — it had not been so one-sided after all. His thoughts had come to her secondhand as it were, but better that than not having known at all.

Her mind began to work faster, searching for a way out of her predicament. An image presented itself — a blonde, about the same age as herself. At the hotel about midweek. An entourage with her. Film starlet, or rich with boyfriends hanging on? Mistaken identity — could that be it? Had she Pippa been taken for the other woman? It was possible.

She addressed the figure before her, beseechingly. 'Please listen to me. I think you've mistaken me for someone else. I've just remembered, there was someone similar to me staying there. She had many people with her. I think she would be rich — very rich. She's the one, not me. I'm the wrong one. Go and look in the hotel during the evening. I'm sure you'll see her.' Then she remembered something and went on hurriedly. 'Tomas would have spoken to her also. All the girls on the beach would speak to him. A handsome man. Please believe me. I came on a package holiday,' she went on, hoping desperately that he would understand. 'Cheaper at this time of the year. Just bed and breakfast. I've saved a long time, just for this holiday, two weeks that's all. Please let me go,' she pleaded. 'I don't know you. I couldn't recognise you again. You've made a terrible mistake. I'm not rich, not worth kidnapping.

'Look,' she said, grabbing her hand-bag from the table, wrenching it open, and tearing the wad of notes from its pocket. She'd had the money put aside for presents. 'There you are — fifty pounds. I've no more.' Pushed it at the figure, her agitated mind not registering the reluctant raising of the hand to take it.

Pippa had the feeling that he was studying her, considering what she had said. She prayed as she had when her father had died, for a release from the first hours of regret, remorse, torment. A different prayer now — in different circumstances. For her own safety, even life.

As he made to leave her she called after him, anger flaring in her. 'Let me go. What's the penalty for kidnapping in your country? Hanging, or life imprisonment? They'll find me, don't you — '
Her voice broke, and then she was alone again.

She sat down, weakly, and with growing alarm. Suppose in the morning they still did not believe her, what would they do? Would they allow her to go? Or . . . Thoughts of what had happened to victims of kidnappers before formed themselves in her mind. But so far they had treated her well, so far . . . she stared at the plain white wall opposite.

She leaned forward, cupped her face in her hands and thoughts floated without effort into her mind. Oh, Tomas, how I could have loved you if things had gone right! They would never believe her at work, that this had happened to her. She'd heard on the

news of this sort of thing happening
— to other people. Watched the victims'
homecoming on television. The strained
faces, the photographers, newsmen.
Their halting stories. Now it was her
turn. She smiled wearily with a trace of
hysteria into the dark of her hands. In
the future what a conversation piece!
Oh yes, I remember the day I was
kidnapped in Portugal! On every
hostess's list Guaranteed to command
attention for a while.

She became aware that someone was
standing in front of her. She looked up
quickly. The hooded kidnapper was
holding a cup out to her. She hesitated.
The hand holding it moved nearer, and
Pippa took the cup. The contents were
hot, and appeared to be tea. She
mustered a smile and a 'Thank you' at
the shadow under the hood.

The figure nodded its acknowledgement then surprised her further by
dropping two tea bags on to the table
before her, before retreating slowly into
the passageway.

Pippa sniffed at the liquid, then took a sip. It was tea, weak and without sugar and not quite enough milk. Might be a trick. But it tasted all right. She would have preferred some sugar, but, she shrugged inwardly, their treatment of her could be worse. She wondered if the man who had just left her was the only member of the gang. But the note had referred to 'we'.

She leaned back on the settee, put both hands around the cup and then realised she was still holding in one the slip of paper handed to her by her captors earlier. On it was what Tomas was said to have called her — 'English rose', and that he liked her. The tea and the words were comforting in their own way.

Two thoughts came, the first straightforward in its presentation by her mind. Not once had money been mentioned. The second thought was not as distinct or obvious. A faint knocking for recognition at the inner door of her mind. Something she ought to know

— had known. Of no importance before, but now . . .

About an hour later she heard the outer door opening. A wave of air from it. The hooded figure came into the room holding something out to her.

It was money — English money, folded untidily. It was her money being returned. Uncaring, she took it. There was something else engaging her mind. That faint knocking on the door of her memory earlier had become a bludgeoning hammer into her consciousness. The hand which had held out the notes to her. Something on it.

No! It could not be. She did not want it to be. Blinding cruel realisation. The ring! She had seen it before. It was all a dream as if standing apart from herself. 'Tomas! take off your hood. Tomas! It's you,' she flung at the figure hoarsely.

The figure stood rigid for a moment facing her, head bent, then began to move slowly away.

'No! Tomas — it is you, I know. The ring, I saw it.'

She grabbed at the hood, unmindful of any danger, could not stop herself. She knew the truth, yet did not want confirmation of it. She failed to grasp the hood completely but her fingers caught sufficient of the material to pull it away from the face.

Like a doll in a musical box he turned slowly, stiffly.

Wide-eyed, she stared at him over her hands, stunned at the truth.

Tomas stared back at her, darker, younger looking in the artificial light.

'Why, Tomas, why?' she whispered.

Calmly Tomas unzipped the top half of the robe, let the garment fall to his feet, then with a certain dignity stepped out of it. Kicked it away.

Pippa gazed at him as if seeing him for the first time. This was not her Tomas, could not be. He would not have done what he had. This Tomas appeared different. The absence of the cap which he used to wear over his eyes, though the ridge of hair was still there. He wore a white open necked shirt under a grey pullover and dark trousers. He had a more sophisticated look about him had this Tomas, without his bulky fisherman's clothes. And yet in a strange way he appeared old-fashioned. As in pictures she'd seen of young men in the Thirties on record sleeves and television plays. An inconsequential thought fluttered through her brain. His stern, composed face looked like those fashioned in pottery and made to hang flat against a wall.

'Why, Tomas?' she repeated tremulously, and saw his searching for words. When they came they were in Portuguese, staccato, direct at her — only a few. She didn't understand. It did not matter. Her heart seemed to shrink inside her. This man around whom she had built such romantic day-dreams, had kidnapped her. Not for love. Not even to enjoy her body. But for money! What a naive, romantic fool she'd been. Her own fault entirely. Nevertheless the bitter, bitter hurt was bared in her eyes for him to see.

She began to talk quietly, tonelessly, her pent up emotions coming out slowly at first. 'You were my fisherman. My man of the sea. My hero. For the first time in my life I thought you were the one. Thought of us. Dreamed.' She shook her head vaguely. 'Knew it could never come to anything in my heart. You didn't know. I loved you. Thinking about you kept me going. Thought you might even rescue me.'

She laughed shortly, a miserable sound. Her words began to come faster like the last of the liquid from a bottle. Her voice rose, at once accusing and self-recriminating. 'You could have left me with that illusion, instead you spoiled it for me. Just for the money — nothing else. A cheap thief. You're just a contemptible, cheap thief. I was yours, and all you wanted was money . . . ' Real anger possessed her. Her eyes blazed blue. 'Take the bloody money.' Threw the bundle at his face. It struck him then broke apart, the separate notes fluttering to the floor.

She felt something in her other hand. It was the note with 'English rose' and 'Tomas like you' on it. 'You liar. Liked me?' She crushed the paper, flung it away from her.

In the momentary silence the crushed ball of paper began to expand and scrape upon the floor as if imbued with the savage cynicism that had replaced her dream. If her eyes had not been blurred with the beginnings of tears she would have caught the agonising look of sadness on Tomas's face as he turned and walked swiftly from the room.

Pippa collapsed on to the settee, the draught from the open apartment door signalling her freedom. But she was drained of energy, overwrought, and reaction had set in due to the sudden ending of her kidnapping.

Her listless eyes saw the bank notes scattered about the floor where they had fallen when she had thrown them at Tomas. There was a faint rumbling from outside the building. A lorry perhaps? Thunder? It meant nothing to her just then. She would make an effort soon, get up and leave. How strange that half an hour ago she was a prisoner praying to be free. Now the world beckoned her to join it again, and the effort seemed too much.

She was aware of the rumbling again, louder, penetrating her distress. The settee vibrated beneath her. Creaking, cracking sounds came, the table began to slide slowly away from her. The floor began to slant downwards in its middle. She tried to stand, to jump away. Fell against the settee. The floor was fast becoming a hole. She screamed. It fell away from her feet. The room was bending, falling apart. Pippa fell with the table, ceiling, doors and settee.

And on one of the fingers of the hands that tore at the rubble until they streamed with blood was a ring. A ring with two circles in the middle of which was the initial T.

4

Pippa came to in the local hospital to the memory of that yawning hole appearing beneath her feet. Still confused as to what had happened, she was told there had been a minor earthquake to the western side of the town. There had been some casualties. She, they told her, had been lucky, suffering nothing more than concussion and bruises. In a day or so she would be well enough to leave. It appeared that the settee had jammed above her, protecting her from other falling masonry.

An earthquake! So that had been the noise she had heard. Other memories returned with a dull hurt of mind and a rising anger alongside it. She had been abducted, the holiday spoiled, and had lost some money. She felt worried, greatly anxious. Not enough money to pay for any charges incurred in the hospital. She must get someone to send a telegram home for money to pay for that, though fortunately she had paid for the holiday accommodation beforehand.

She raised her head to look at the nurse standing at the bedside. Something touched and caught in her hair. She felt for it with her hand, brought the object into view. Regarded it in great surprise. A rose! A single rose, orange coloured in the middle, deep red on the outer . . . Discreetly scented. Pippa glanced at her bedside table. There were no flowers upon it. It had not fallen from there. Where had it come from? Who had placed it upon her pillow? She held it upright on her breast, twisting its stem between her fingers — a splash of colour against the white sheet.

She endeavoured to find out from the nurse who had brought it. She was told a man. A young Portuguese. Very worried and in such hurry. He had asked for it to be put on her pillow. Describing him, the nurse's face showed her approval of that person. The eyes in the brown face twinkling knowingly and kindly at the romantic episode. Tomas had been the name.

Tomas! Pippa's hand clenched about the rose. Tomas, coming there. When it was all his fault. Kidnapper — thief. The bloody cheek — his nerve! Did he think a rose would put it all right again? What did he think she was? A child to be humoured by a coloured toy to forget so easily. Upset and bitter, her temper flared. Her hand crushed the rose, flung it across the bed to the floor, the flash of sudden anger in the northern blue eyes startling the nurse.

'I want the police, fetch the police. Quickly. Get them here. I must tell them' Pippa demanded. Gone were romantic emotions and thoughts of love. Fresh in her mind was the fright, the great hole through which she had dropped.

Puzzled and somewhat alarmed the

nurse hurried off to seek advice on the English girl calling urgently for the police to be summoned.

Minutes later a small group of hospital staff surrounded her bed, anxious to comfort the patient obviously worried about something. She had not to worry, they said. Clothes would be found for her. Money? Well — several shrugs — something would be done. They were sorry she had lost some of hers. It was possible that it would be found in the rubble. They shook their heads at her. She was lucky to be alive.

But Pippa was adamant, she must see the police. She had something very important to tell them. The group moved away in serious muted discussion with occasional backward glances in her direction.

The result of all this was indeed a visit the following morning from the police — an older man in plain clothes and a young policeman dressed in the customary grey uniform. Both appeared to be taken with her, the older man with an eye to feminine beauty of the fair type, and the younger unable to restrain his eyes from wandering occasionally to the form outlined beneath the light covering sheets.

Pippa wasted no time, plunging straight into her story in angry and bitter tones, addressing herself to the older man. How she had been going to meet Tomas. The taking of her to the apartment, the keeping of her there, ransom money. The hooded figure and the fact that she had recognised him by the ring on his finger.

The plain clothes policeman listened patiently, occasionally shooting a question at his constable as if seeking confirmation on some part of Pippa's story.

When she had finished, he asked in good English, 'You say you had met this Tomas before?'

'Yes, on the beach several times. I used to take a stroll there most mornings.'

'And he asked you to meet him that day?'

'Yes.'

'You liked this Tomas?'

'Yes, I did.'

'Very much?'

'More than any other man I had ever met.' She felt as if she were rehearsing a play — saying lines written by someone else.

'He did not meet you as arranged, but someone else did instead?'

'Yes, he said he'd take me to Tomas, and he did,' she added bitterly.

The policeman gave an almost imperceptible nod as if satisfied with his own thoughts. He went on, 'What would you say if I told you that this Tomas — he is a fisherman, yes? — ' Pippa nodded, 'that this Tomas was the one that rescued you from the collapsed building?'

Disbelief, then amazement showed through her smouldering anger. Not waiting for her to speak the policeman continued, 'Those there have said he

71

was like a madman, tearing at the stones, calling for you. The strength of a bull. His hands were torn.'

'Are you sure?' she whispered. Her mind was turning upside down. Tried to remember. He had left just before the quake occurred. He could still have been in the near vicinity. Some anger reasserted itself in her. 'Well, that proves that he was nearby at least.'

'Yes,' said the other, 'but that also does not prove that he kidnapped you.'

'But how do you know that he rescued me?' she queried.

'The ambulance people. They saw him. He carried you to it, insisted on accompanying you to the hospital. They had to treat his hands.'

'Very well,' she said grudgingly, 'he got me out,' then added resentfully, 'but he did kidnap me. He should be punished.' She paused for breath, went on vehemently, 'after all, why should I have been in the apartment if I hadn't been kidnapped and taken there? I am on holiday and staying at the Monte Sirrocco Hotel.'

The plain clothes policeman stared silently at her. Made a slight grimace, turned his hands palm upwards. 'The days have been hot — perhaps you are not used to the heat. It is possible you wandered up there.' He shrugged. 'Cool and quiet.'

Pippa, taut during her accusations, now slumped deep in her pillow. They didn't understand. Doubt on the older man's face, the other she didn't think understood any English. There was no proof of anything she had told them. She couldn't prove anything. Anyway, it didn't matter now.

After they'd gone she lay quietly, drained of energy, too tired even to think and before long drifted into sleep. A nurse came along, picked up the crushed rose from the floor, looked at it and wondered.

★   ★   ★

The next morning Pippa was discharged and taken back to her hotel. She was glad and relieved to be inside it again. The foyer was busy yet with an air of calm and orderliness, the reception staff smart with their fawn suits and short hair. They were helpful and sympathetic towards her, expressing their wonderment that she had survived the catastrophe that had befallen part of Allemura. Pippa guessed that they knew nothing about the kidnapping, but presumed that she had been sight-seeing in that area of the town when the earth tremor occurred.

The cashier was quick to allay her anxieties regarding the loss of her money, and assured her that everything would be arranged in the next few hours if she would let them have the name of her bank in England. In the meantime, he said the hotel would be glad to provide her lunch and anything she wanted — hairdressing, sauna, clothes cleaning, free of charge.

Pippa knew that she looked a sight

— she was wearing the same dress she had been kidnapped in. It was torn and dirty and a light blanket loaned from the hospital was draped over her shoulders.

Just before she was taken up to her room the cashier handed her a sealed and bulky looking envelope. It had been delivered early that morning. Pippa regarded it, puzzled. Just her full name care of the hotel written in block capitals upon it.

Alone in her room she sat on her bed and opened the package. Portuguese bank notes folded neatly inside it. A slip of paper fluttered to the bed. On it was written one word. '*Tomas*'. She shrank inwardly, momentarily, the unpleasantness associated with his name still fresh in her mind. Looked at the address again. It was definitely for her, from him. She gazed at the money for a few moments greatly surprised, then in a strangely disinterested fashion roughly counted the notes. There was the equivalent of fifty pounds.

She got up from the bed, began to run the bath water, ignoring her image in the large mirror in the bathroom, threw off her clothes. She didn't want to see them again. The bruises were still dark upon her body. She could have been paralysed, in a wheelchair, or dead. And all because of one thieving fisherman.

She stirred the water with her foot — stepped in. She herself had been at fault also. So naïve and girlish as to be almost unbelievable. Truly she had acted like a stupid idiot. Nevertheless that did not excuse the act that he had perpetuated against her.

Pippa lay back in the water, closed her eyes and the world outside seemed far away for the present, and in the comforting, caressing warmth of her bath Pippa's attitude towards Tomas began to change slowly. She remembered the rose from him on her pillow in the hospital, and had he not had to have treatment to his hands from the effort of pulling her from the ruins? He could have raced away and left her, no one would have known that she had been in the building. Instead he had risked being found out, and perhaps more serious injury to himself in order to rescue her.

Other things that had been mentioned now came back to her. Like a madman — such great strength in order to get her out of the collapsed building. And he had carried her to the ambulance and remained with her all the time to the hospital. Now the money he had sent. He was trying to make up for what he had done to her.

She got out of the bath, began to dry herself, her thoughts still busy. In the hospital when she had called for the police she had been shocked, angry and bitter. Had wanted to hurt Tomas, see him punished. Now it did not seem to matter so much. The episode was over and done with. The police hadn't really believed her story anyway.

Pippa dared to look at herself in the mirror. Her face was thinner, the signs

77

of strain still evident in her eyes and round her mouth. But considering what she had gone through she thought that she was not looking too bad.

Later, dressed in clean fresh clothes and sipping a late morning coffee in her room she began to think that life was worth living after all. She must rejoin that life, not sit in her bedroom all day feeling sorry for herself. The sounds of splashing and laughter and conversation came from the pool below her balcony. She had not used it a lot during her holiday, preferring to go to the beach. Perhaps later in the afternoon she would go down for a swim.

How many days of her holiday had she left? It was now Thursday. That left two full days, her plane leaving late Saturday afternoon. There was no time to lose, she must make the most of the remainder of her holiday. She decided to lunch in the hotel restaurant, and whilst downstairs see if the cashier had come to some arrangement with her bank.

78

Pippa glanced at the money on the bed again. She could always pay for anything else that she wanted with some of that. But she was uneasy about the money that Tomas had sent. If she could do without it she would. It wasn't hers — she had thrown hers away. She told herself not to be so stupid, that it was hers — And yet . . .

5

The next morning she was down early for breakfast, joining the few people already scattered about the large dining room. The breakfast waiters looked at her with interest and those with some grasp of English enquired after her health. One or two of the more senior waiters she had seen the night before at dinner. Then, they had been smiling and handsome in the candlelight, pouring the wine. Now at breakfast, they looked wan and serious in their supervision of the first meal of the day. They were a different type, not like Tomas. She sipped at her coffee — having had tea in her room earlier. She was surprised to find herself thinking about him, and out of habit glanced out of the large windows and across the pool to the road beyond leading to the beach. Would he be there as usual as if nothing had happened?

She finished her breakfast quickly and went to the cashier's desk in the foyer. He was busy with someone else, but afterwards he recognised her immediately and she guessed from his beaming smile that all was well.

'Good morning, Miss Gentle, it is settled. Your bank has co-operated. One hundred pounds, will that be sufficient?'

Pippa was relieved. 'Yes, oh, yes, thank you very much. I feel better about the matter now. I was worried — I didn't know how I was going to pay for things.'

He shrugged, smiling. 'Now it is all right, eh?' He counted it out in Portuguese money.

It came to slightly more than she had expected. Good old England, she thought, the exchange rate was up in its favour.

'There,' the cashier said with a slight flourish, 'Now you will be able to buy your presents to take home with you.'

Presents! She'd forgotten all about them in the strange happenings of the previous few days. 'I wish it was sunshine I could take back,' she returned cheerily. 'Thank you very much for everything.'

'We try to help. Bom dia.'

'B — bom dia,' Pippa tried.

She made straight for her room, the swift, silent and nearly jerk-free lift making it easy. Once there she placed half the money she had just obtained in her suitcase and the other half in her handbag alongside that given to her by Tomas. For a moment she looked at the two wads of notes. Then she took Tomas's and tucked it into a separate compartment in the handbag. Somehow she felt that she wanted to keep it apart — not to use any of it. She had the equivalent of fifty pounds of her own for presents, more than enough, and the other fifty in her suitcase to pay for anything else before she left, and for drinks and so on at the airport. She smiled rather shamefacedly to herself.

She liked a drink occasionally, but the one time when she did indulge was when she took a plane anywhere. Nerves — but the drink helped.

It was a quarter past ten when she walked down the street from the hotel and for the first time by herself since the day she had been kidnapped. It was pleasant under the morning sun and not too hot, and she had some re-tanning to do before Saturday, otherwise she would go back as pale as she had arrived.

It was a good thing that the cashier had mentioned presents — she had completely forgotten about them. One for her mother, brother, sister-in-law and their children. And one or two for friends.

She reached the crossroads, having a strange feeling that it was like beginning a short holiday all over again. Pre-kidnap, post-kidnap, she thought wryly. She turned along the road leading to the pottery shop — she would see what they had there. Perhaps nothing for the children, but no doubt something for the adults.

It was pleasant at the pottery, cool and crammed from floor to ceiling with colourful ceramics of all designs and sizes. Two young men about her own age were busy painting newly made earthenware, occasionally putting aside their work to serve a customer.

Once Pippa glanced up to see the interested gaze of one upon her. He said something to the other who looked up and Pippa hoped that whatever had been said was complimentary. While not yet back to her best, she felt that she was not the dishevelled wreck of forty-eight hours before.

She made her purchases including a coffee set for her mother comprising of a jug and six cups, with the outside of each piece covered with the bark of a tree. She had nothing yet for her nieces, but was sure she would find something suitable in the village.

Setting off back towards the cross-roads, she passed the place where she had waited for Tomas last Tuesday. Was it only so little time ago? She was reminded of the money in her bag, the money that he had sent. Her watch said five minutes past eleven. Time for a coffee. She would finish off her shopping later.

She turned right at the crossroads, her breathing quickening. Straight there and back, she told herself. Coffee, then return the money to him and away again. He may not be there — what then? She would perhaps be able to leave it with someone who knew him, at the restaurant itself. If not she would keep it, knowing that she had tried to return it.

Pippa was hardly aware of the passing holidaymakers, the small busy market on the street side, the nearness of the occasional car. A hotel pool — a glimpse of colours around it beyond the screening trees. Suppose he was there. What should she say? Very little, she thought. Would be dignified, aloof. Hand it over, and leave.

The road began its descent to the beach. A coffee first or . . . Her thoughts were becoming indecisive, muddled. Dependent on whether he was there or not. What the hell? Why bother? He had kidnapped her. She was crazy. Wasn't even sure now that she wanted to see him again.

She rounded a corner. Before her lay the spread of blue sea and part of the beach, but the one with the fishing boats on it still hidden from her sight by the restaurant terrace. Towels fluttered from the apartment balconies nearby, tops of umbrellas, and quiet lazy contented conversation. Dark figures against the sand, and water.

The terrace was busy, and she threaded her way slowly between the tables to the railings overlooking the beach. The line of boats. Her eyes slid over them quickly and back again. No Tomas. Disappointment gripped her. The boat was there, though, almost straight ahead. She shielded her eyes against the glare and stared hard at it.

Over the stern and curving sides to the prow. A thin dark line at its front smudging its colours.

Something moved against the blue. Suddenly she realised what it was. A man's head. Someone was standing with their back against the rearing prow of the boat, his head moving occasionally. The darker strip near the front against the bright paint was his clothing. In a flash her mood had changed. Was it Tomas? She began to make her way off the terrace, trying to keep her eyes on the front of the boat. Stumbled against a table, apologised unseeingly to those seated at it. When she looked again the figure had gone, the full line of the boat paintwork visible. There was no sign of anyone who looked like Tomas. Just one elderly man attending to a boat at the far end of the row.

She hurried past the back of the wooden kiosk, down the side of it towards the steps. A fisherman was coming up them. She gasped out loud.

It was Tomas. Knew before he lifted his head.

He stopped dead a third of the way up, hand on the rail. Her own was white as she gripped the wood, and stood looking down on him. Both instantly frozen in motion — a still photograph.

But Pippa's emotions were in flood. In a million years she would love him. Nothing had changed for her. No matter what he did she would love him. Blue jerseyed, grey trousers rolled up and barefoot. The flat cap no longer able to shadow his face as he gazed upwards. The plastered fingers. Fleeting seconds for her to see the amazement, then joy flitting across his features, matching her own.

He stepped backwards, his expression settling into one of glad wariness.

'Good morning.' It came out stiffly. She knew it was, but had not intended it to be.

'Bom,' he began, 'good morning.'

She noticed that he had not added

her name, just as she had not spoken his.

He moved to the bottom of the steps, making a courtly gesture with his arm for her to descend. The dark eyes observed her closely as she went down slowly.

She tapped at the bag which she was clutching. 'I have something for you.' It was a relief to speak again.

They faced each other on the sand.

'I wait every day for the police to come for me,' he said matter of factly. 'I think you must tell them you know me.' He moved a shell with his foot, glanced beyond her, then regarded her again.

She observed how large and brown his eyes were, now that he was not squinting into the sun. Just for a moment she wanted to say that she had told the police, to see him worried, fearful. Instead she lied. 'No, I did not tell them,' and wondered if he'd heard from someone that she had indeed called for the police when she was in hospital.

He touched his eyes with his finger tips. 'I do not sleep since,' he said with the vestige of a smile.

'And so you should not after what you did,' she retorted severely, her blue eyes smouldering for an instant, but then betraying something of what she felt for him. She was somewhat embarrassed, having said things to him in frightened temper at the apartment. She had revealed her innermost feelings towards him. But yet, hadn't he revealed something of what he felt for her? His having the rose put on her pillow, and his frantic efforts to rescue her, witnessed by others.

'I not think you come here again.' His voice was deep but soft like the murmuring of the sea beyond them. That and the accent had appealed to her when they had first spoken together.

'I would not have come, but I had to bring you this.' She delved into her bag, brought out the envelope with the money in it. Pushed it at him. 'The money you sent to me at the hotel, I don't want it. It's yours — not mine.'

Tomas looked surprised, but his hands remained at his side. She touched his sleeve with the envelope. 'Take it please,' she insisted.

He took it only to hold it out immediately to her in return. 'For your holiday and dress — spoiled.'

She took a step back. 'No,' she said firmly, 'The hotel people have arranged enough for me to manage on until I get home. Some arrangement with my bank. Though I shall have precious little left when I do get back.'

He looked puzzled, regarded her intently. 'I give all the money back to you — you remember?' She saw something akin to shame pass across his face.

Pippa nodded. 'Yes, you did, but then I threw it back at you.' She blushed at the memory and at what she had called him. It had been deserved at the time. Now in the sun and face to face again the whole affair seemed almost funny — almost, but not quite.

Tomas continued to stare at her, his eyes seeming to look into her mind.

'Before I could pick it up again, the whole place fell apart,' she explained. For a moment the horror of it returned and her feelings must have communicated themselves to the man before her. His eyes widening in understanding — a realisation of what she had gone through. Shook his head slowly, muttered something sharply which she did not understand.

He thrust the envelope at her. 'You take this, important. You have no money, I get more for you.'

She stepped away, exclaiming determinedly, 'No, it was my fault. You gave it to me, I lost it. I'm all right, got enough to last now until I get home.'

The thought came that if passers-by saw him pressing the money upon her, they would think that she had a different profession from that of typist.

To her surprise he dropped the envelope to the ground. 'Then I let it lie. I not take it. You English — stubborn.' He spoke quietly, finally. His eyes challenging hers.

'Well, we may be stubborn, but at least we do not kidnap visitors to our country,' she retorted coldly, and saw his eyelids flicker as her words went home.

His gaze dropped away, a withdrawn expression suddenly appearing. He nodded, looking at the sand, laughed shortly. 'Yes, a terrible thing. I did terrible thing to you.' He paused then regarded her again. 'Never will you forgive me, I know.' He stated it simply, flatly — resignedly. He half turned towards the steps.

Suddenly Pippa realised she was going to lose him forever in a few seconds. He had taken it to heart, he was sorry. It was in his face. But if she let him go now she would never see him again. Out of her life forever. She must not allow that to happen. 'Wait, Tomas,' she exclaimed hastily. It was the first time that she had called him by his name since their conversation began. 'I can forgive. Please.' Her fingers touched his sleeve. If she made a fool of herself now it did not matter. He waited, eyes fixed on her face, seeming to read into her soul.

'I didn't just come,' she went on, 'to return that money. I — I came because I wanted to thank you for rescuing me and — and — for the rose,' she gave a half smile, 'you remember, in the hospital.'

Tomas's look had softened at her words. 'You found it?'

She nodded. 'Yes, it was sweet and kind of you, and very risky. You might have been caught.'

He shrugged with a wry smile. 'Maybe I deserved it, eh?'

She did not answer, her eyes resting on him. Two days ago, he certainly would have deserved it. Now . . .

He lifted his cap, then reseated it in almost exactly the same position. She saw the scar high on his forehead which had hitherto been hidden. It looked a recent injury. She noticed his plastered fingers again.

'Your head and fingers, what have you done?' She knew well enough but not knowing quite what else to say to continue the conversation.

He glanced down at his hands then regarded her steadily, his face intently serious, but she was surprised to see the devils dancing in the depth of his eyes. 'Digging for a girl called Peepa, who once called me a thief. You think me still a thief?' The dancing lights were faintly mocking now.

Pippa saw the envelope between them on the ground, sand already upon it. Shook her head gently, did not look at him.

He sighed — a deep, consciously over-acted movement spreading to outstretched hands. 'Then we friends again — eh?'

She nodded her assent, managing a smile. Friends! She was in love — never been out of it despite her experiences at his hands. It was Friday and she would leave on Saturday. How could friends become something much more before then? Impossible, it was farcical.

Tomas reached out and grasped her hand, then turned gently pulling her with him. 'We sit up here,' he nodded upwards at the kiosk, 'more comfortable.' He led her up the steps her hand in his.

Pippa glanced down at her hand encased in his. It was the first time they had touched each other properly. His skin was a dark gold, the forearm thick like a young tree trunk. Black hairs dense towards the wrist. Were men closer to the animals? She wanted to touch the growth with her free hand.

Then she saw the envelope still lying on the sand. 'The money, Tomas, don't leave it.'

He looked back at her, then stopped and shrugged. 'You must not leave it,' he said pointedly.

She looked at him in some exasperation, decided not to argue with him. She bent and picked it up, then, still holding on to him, followed him up the steps.

They sat side by side in the shade of the kiosk's veranda. It reminded her of a neglected miniature cricket pavilion. Somehow sitting down seemed to give their relationship a more permanent air.

Tomas leaned back against the wood, regarded her sideways from under his cap. 'We talk about you now, not me. You better after hospital?'

She discerned a faint note of concern. Smiled at him briefly. 'Yes, thank you.' She did not want to discuss anything relating to the affair, and hoped he would pass on to another topic.

But he persisted. 'You brave woman, Pippa. You have fuego.' Saw her blank look. 'Fire,' he explained, 'magnificent in temper.' His tone was teasing but his look was admiring.

'I did not feel very brave,' she said quietly. Then suddenly irritated by his manner she asked bluntly, 'D'you make a habit of kidnapping people?'

He seemed in no way put about, regarding her a moment, then a slow smile breaking, humour kindling in his eyes. 'Young and beautiful ladies, yes.'

She ignored the easy compliment, looked away from him, thinking he would certainly have the pick of the women who came down to that beach.

She worked her teeth on her lip. Wanted to find out more about him. She knew so little. Glancing at him she saw that he had been about to say something and wondered what it was. Instead, he stretched his legs out in front of him.

'Are your parents alive, Tomas?' she asked.

He looked surprised, nodded.

'D'you live with them?'

'No.'

Perhaps he resented her questions?

He drew his legs up, leaned forward elbows on knees and spoke at the distant sea. 'I live alone, Pippa. Away from them. It is sad but necessary. All things living leave home.' He shrugged.

'Natural.' Turned to look at her. 'Cannot kiss girls in front of parents.'

She saw the mischievous lights dancing in his eyes. He did not laugh much, but the humour bubbled near the surface. Again she had to remind herself that this was the same man who had kidnapped her.

He turned fully towards her, leaning on his hand and she saw that he had become suddenly very serious, his eyes unfathomable in their brown depths. 'You remember, Pippa, in the apartment,' he began. How could she forget? She wondered what was coming. 'You say many things to me,' he went on, 'some bad — some good.' She waited, her gaze locked with his. 'Did you mean the good thing?'

Pippa knew what he was trying to say. In her fear and hurt, she had flung abuse at him, but also she had said other things — the truth had come out. How she had loved him from afar, the good thing he had mentioned. Still did so. Her eyes moved away from him slowly, her throat felt dry. 'Yes, I did.'

Tomas got up, stood looking out over the veranda rail. She couldn't see his expression. Noticed the muscle standing out on his arm as he gripped the wood. She sighed inwardly. He knew her feelings towards him. What had he given in return? He liked her, yes, though even that he had not actually said to her. It was so one sided. Knowing what he did he should have taken her in his arms. Perhaps he delighted in twisting a woman's emotions, catching his prey then losing interest.

In a detached way she watched two children down in the water playing with a rubber dinghy, trying to clamber into it as it rose steeply to the waves. Happy cries, laughter — she guessed Tomas was looking down at them also.

'You like children, Pippa?' he asked, still looking out over the beach.

'Oh, yes, I'd love to fill a house with them.' His question had surprised her, but her answer was truthful. Work had

100

not been easy to get recently back home, and she had taken the job of typist, but would have liked to have been a children's nurse. Such a position had not been available at the time, though, and with her father passing away, she had had to help to support her mother.

'Fill a house with them?' Tomas echoed, half turned towards her, but still gazing into the distance. Pippa detected a tolerant amusement in his voice.

'Yes, from babies up to seven-year-olds. They're lovely then, unspoilt, innocent, trusting, believing in what you tell them.'

She realised that she, too, had been trusting, believing this man standing in front of her, yet she would gladly fill his house with their children.

She smiled inwardly remembering her father saying to her mother in a moment of desperate exasperation that the first thirty years were the worst when bringing up children.

She became aware that he had turned towards her, leaning with his back against the rail. Could not see his expression clearly, it being in shadow, but guessed that he was eyeing her.

He pointed to the bag holding her presents. 'You have been shopping?'

She looked down, had almost forgotten about it. 'Yes, I visited the pottery shop earlier, but I've still one or two things to get.'

'When d'you fly to England?' His tone was polite — faintly interested.

She thought it was like the brief conversation of strangers on a station platform, never likely to see each other again.

'Tomorrow — half past five,' she replied dully. Suddenly an irrational surge of anger overcame her. Why couldn't everything have gone smoothly for her? Why could it not have ended as it should have done? No kidnapping, no trouble, just fully in love together. Marriage. A home in England or in Portugal. Her mother to spend some time with them, some with her brother. Happiness, no problem.

'What is wrong?' Tomas's voice broke into her thoughts. He sat down but nearer to her this time. 'Your face,' his hand described a circle in front of his own. 'I see sad Pippa.' He was observing her closely.

'I don't want to go back to England yet,' she sighed the words.

'To the rain, eh?'

She nodded, looking away to the sea thinking that was not true. She was used to the rain and the winter. No, going home meant leaving Tomas. She wanted to remain because of him.

'Then you stay here in Portugal.'

Pippa turned to him sharply, then realised her eagerness had no doubt given her real thoughts away. His regard of her was deep, steady. Was he serious? His expression gave nothing away.

'Wish I could,' she murmured, looking away, but conscious of his gaze still upon her. In the years to come, she thought, she would remember the

Algarve, that most beautiful place. Remember it with an ache in her heart. As a place where the sun-warmed gentle breeze whispered that the man sitting next to her could never be hers. Perhaps in time the ache would diminish.

She turned to him again. The dark mat of hair rising to the base of his throat. Oh, if only she could wind her arms around him, fingers caressing his head, then for them to slip down and palm those on his chest. To hear his words 'I love you.'

She saw a small frown appear, looked as if he were about to say something, glanced at his feet, then almost immediately a more determined regard of her returned. 'I like you to see my boat, we go for a sail,' he said waving an arm at the horizon. 'Sea very calm you not be seasick.' He waited expectantly.

Pippa stared at him, didn't know whether to laugh or cry. So she did both, could not help the tears welling up. Shook her head slowly in wonder.

This was just where she'd come in — a lifetime away but in reality only a few days ago she'd waited for him to take her to the boat.

Tomas's frown had deepened, narrow eyes questioning hers in puzzled concern.

To see his etchings — she began to laugh quietly. He wouldn't understand.

She knew she was behaving stupidly with a mild hysteria. She leaned back against the warm wood of the kiosk, her shoulders shaking. After a few moments she calmed down, glanced at him. 'Don't mind me, Tomas. Not your fault, something I just thought of. Couldn't help myself. I'm all right now.' She patted her dress pocket for a handkerchief. Must be in her bag. She reached for it.

Tomas's hand rested on her shoulder. Its warmth striking through and bathing her heart. He leaned towards her, caressing her eyes with a big dark red handkerchief as lightly as a hovering butterfly on a summer flower.

She acknowledged his concerned and tender act. 'Thanks, Tomas, and I'd like very much to come for a sail with you — love to see your boat.'

She paused, seeing how her answer had transformed his features. The glowing pleasure in his eyes, the glint of white teeth in the beginning of a smile. 'But when, Tomas? I've only this afternoon and tomorrow morning — that's all.'

Tomas stood up, offered his hand to her, brown eyes gleaming. 'Now. I take you now. Plenty of time, then we eat later.'

Pippa took his hand to rise in delighted surprise. Then bent, and with her free hand grasped her handbag and the other with her presents in it. Just then a woman came round the corner of the kiosk.

Tomas let go of her hand, and Pippa looked up. She was shocked at the bolt of bared jealousy emanating from the eyes staring into her own over Tomas's shoulder. The woman and Tomas began to talk in what Pippa guessed was Portuguese. The woman angrily at first with a nod of the head in her direction, then gradually more calmly. Her looks at Tomas and the little touches she gave on his arm, his face, were proprietory. He was no stranger to her, nor she to him obviously. She was dressed in white including a large wide brimmed hat shading the dark strikingly beautiful features. The dress appeared moulded to a body in which every movement suggested highly charged sexuality.

Most men would be attracted to her, Pippa thought and was gripped by a jealousy of her own. One of Tomas's girl friends, one of many — no doubt. She felt as if she had been forgotten. Saw Tomas shake his head at something the woman said, then glance back with a reassuring smile. Pippa stood up, found her own handkerchief from her handbag and dabbed the remaining dampness from the corners of her eyes. Remembered how he had done that for her a few minutes before. How sweet and concerned of him. But did it mean anything? She glanced in their direction — they were still talking together.

Suddenly the conversation finished and Tomas turned to her, pointed to the beach. 'I fetch sandals — I forget,' he said and went off quickly down the steps.

The woman hesitated a moment then faced Pippa with a look of sullen satisfaction but clearly annoyed at his departure and the end of their conversation. 'You cry, I see. Tomas make many girls cry, you not know him, better that you do not. You be unhappy. You forget him after holiday eh?' A cold little smile showed. The eyes were stony brown orbs in full circles of white.

It was a warning, hands off, Pippa knew. She spoke with an assurance she did not feel, glad of the discomfiture caused to the other by Tomas's abrupt departure to the beach. 'I wasn't crying because of sadness. It was relief, happiness.' It sounded silly but it was true, and whether the woman opposite understood or not, didn't matter.

The woman in white shrugged and ran a dismissive eye over Pippa, the latter feeling flat and insipid in comparison though she was the slightly taller of the two. 'How long you stay on holiday?' she asked.

Pippa shrugged — she was getting the habit. 'I don't know, I haven't decided yet.' She felt a wicked pleasure at seeing the other's irritation.

'You leave Portugal quick,' said the other jerking her head backwards towards the beach. 'He no good for you.'

But good for you, thought Pippa, then saw Tomas returning up the steps.

The girl in white flung a flurry of words at him to which he paid no attention, and she with a final malicious glance at Pippa brushed past her and out of sight round the corner of the kiosk.

6

Tomas brushed the sand from his feet, stepped into his sandals and bent to fasten them. He reminded Pippa of a coiled spring — with a compressed and hidden strength. Then he took her hand and she followed. He glanced back at her. 'What did Carmella say?'

Carmella. The other woman. It suited her, thought Pippa. A luscious scented name. She half shrugged. 'Oh, nothing much. She didn't seem very pleased with me. Asked me when I was going back home.'

Tomas did not pass any comment and they walked past the terrace. Further up the road the girl Carmella was just getting into a white expensive looking sports car and Pippa watched as she roared away up the hill, accelerating fiercely.

'She thinks she owns me,' said Tomas

gazing after the fast disappearing car. 'Wants me to see her today. I tell her I take you instead. Little time for me to see you, Pippa.'

'Don't you like her?' asked Pippa.

Gullies formed on his forehead, his shoulders moved as he looked sideways at her. 'Not enough. She talks always of marriage.' He began to lead her across the road to a battered looking, small yellow car.

Obviously, he was frightened off by talk of marriage, thought Pippa. Perhaps he did not like the Carmella woman enough to marry her, but the fact was that he probably would be the same at the mention of marriage with anybody, and that included herself. And why not? He had everything, no doubt. Feminine company when he wanted it, his freedom and his boat. Why seek the ties of marriage?

Tomas held the car door open for her and she got in wondering how many more girls had sat there before her. He slid into the driving seat, tapped the steering wheel. 'Old car, but it goes where I drive.' His smile at her held the vestige of an apology.

'Well, that's all that matters, Tomas, so long as it gets you around,' she said, anxious to allay any unease he felt. Actually the car had seen many better days unlike that which the girl Carmella had driven away. Suddenly for some reason she felt dispirited. Perhaps the girl Carmella had caused it. She, Pippa, was clinging to straws, being foolish again. Would have been better to have stayed away from the beach and Tomas. Opening the wound in her heart all over again.

Tomas started the engine, pulled at the peak of his cap and put the gear lever forward.

'We are going to see your boat now are we, Tomas?' Pippa asked, hesitating fractionally over his name.

He turned to her. 'You think of getting out if I say no?' His eyes held a challenging, mocking gleam.

She felt her cheeks warming, not all

due to the heat. He had guessed what had passed through her mind. 'No, of course not, I'm looking forward to seeing it.'

Tomas gave a small definite nod of the head. 'Then I take you.'

They set off up the hill with a rising note from the car's exhaust and Pippa thinking that she had a right to feel a certain apprehension after what had happened earlier in the week. That awakened another question in her mind. Why had Tomas not kidnapped the girl Carmella? She was obviously far from poor, probably from a rich Portuguese family. If he had wanted money he would have been more likely to have obtained it from her or her parents.

Pippa's thoughts ran on. Perhaps the very fact that Carmella was Portuguese and her parents influential and able to bring more pressure to bear on the police to catch any kidnapper had made Tomas decide on someone with whom the risk of detection would be less.

She saw that they had now turned into the road leading to Allemura and wondered how far it was to where he kept his boat. It was somewhere near the town, she knew. She stole a glance at his profile, almost stern in its expression as he concentrated on keeping the little car on course over the dusty uneven road. Observed the strong forearms, the muscles outlined in constant rippling movement. Her glance slipped to his hands, saw the ring again. The sight of it gave her a feeling of unreality. Was it little more than two days since she had recognized that ring as being his in the apartment? And yet here they were together on the way to see his boat.

As they neared Allemura Pippa could not prevent her gaze from lifting to the far upper side of the town. She could make out the broken, collapsed buildings, the yellow movement of bulldozers and lorries. She became aware that Tomas was addressing her — his voice raised above the bustle and

114

noise of the town.

'Better a Rolls-Royce for you.' She caught his admiring glance — took pleasure in his implied compliment.

She smiled at him as he guided the car down towards the main square. 'I'm enjoying the ride in this.' What she really wanted to tell him was that he was the important thing, not the car. Saw his mouth corners twitch upwards and was glad he had broken the silence between them, he having had a preoccupied air during the latter part of the journey. His admiration worked wonders for her, she beginning to feel much more cheerful and confident by the minute, though the outfit she was wearing was nothing special, she thought, a white flared skirt, and a blue and white hooped sleeveless top, and sandals. Perhaps she looked well because she was with the man she loved. That time was precious — must be enjoyed to the full. The future was in two days.

They entered the main square and

turned left, driving along between the many buses, taxis and motor scooters, Tomas bringing the car to rest in a small, relatively peaceful square at its far end. He got out and opened the door for her. Whatever else he might be, she thought, he was polite in an old-fashioned way. She was aware of his gaze moving over her, hesitating a moment on her cleavage, then rising to her face. Then he led her up the short street towards the beach. Passed the few people on the orange seats outside the corner café.

Pippa recognised that particular beach — it being known as Fisherman's beach. She had walked along it once before. On that occasion she had reached it by way of the tunnel from the town centre, and had then walked around at low tide. The nearby fish market was busy with the new catch, tourists and locals alike looking on. Older fishermen leaning on the sea wall, younger ones attending to their boats and nets strung out along the sand.

Tomas motioned at the market. 'I catch some of that.' There was a note of pride in his voice. She noticed his nods to a few fishermen but he did not stop to talk. And Pippa had a feeling that although Tomas was a fisherman like them, there was something about him that was different — set him apart.

Reaching the beach itself they began to walk across it, his hand seeking hers as soon as they were clear of the bustling activity. They walked in silence, Pippa noticing a frown on her companion's brow, he appearing deep in concentrated thought.

They came to a line of rocks which diminished in height towards the water, and Pippa felt his hand tighten on hers. Rounding the rocks, she saw they were on a small, sheltered beach, the land behind high enough to make it private.

'There.' His hand pointed hers. A hundred yards out was a boat whose hull was the colour of the sky that day — brilliant blue with a white cabin top. A strip of white showed the furled sail along its boom. It rode quietly, its anchor chain slanting to the water.

'It's beautiful, Tomas.'

For a few moments he stared at the craft appraising it critically with narrowed seaman's eyes, and Pippa felt that she had been forgotten. Then he turned away nodding his satisfaction and made his way up the beach to a small rowing boat whose rope was fastened to a ring embedded in one of the larger rocks. Untying this he then pulled the boat down to the water's edge.

He shot a glance of humour at her. 'Not swim, too far, Pippa.'

She smiled. 'Yes, I'd rather the boat if you don't mind, Tomas.'

How easy it was becoming to speak his name. She was losing that awkwardness that she had felt earlier on renewing their acquaintance. She slipped off her sandals.

He pushed the boat into the water until it floated, stood holding it for her, then handed her in to it, and a minute later he was pulling hard away from the shore.

As they drew nearer to the boat, Pippa realised that it was larger than she had first thought. Guessed its length at about twenty-five feet. Small waves lapped and dimpled its white water line. She could not see a name upon it. Perhaps he had not christened it yet.

Tomas went aboard first then helped Pippa clamber after him, an act which she felt she accomplished with little dignity, almost falling into the cockpit. She straightened her clothing and laughed rather self-consciously. 'You can see I'm not used to boats.'

Tomas shrugged with a kindly amusement. 'No matter, you here in my boat — very good,' and set her down carefully on one of the side seats.

She watched as he went forward taking a key from his pocket and unlocking the polished wood cabin door. In the gloom of the cabin interior Pippa discerned a large bunk, the width of the forward part of the boat. Nearer the door opening was a small cooker. Suddenly she felt apprehensive. Had she been naïve again, a fool to come aboard the boat alone with him? He'd kidnapped her once, he could do it again.

Tomas glanced back at her. Did he guess her thoughts? 'Sea calm, you not worry, Pippa — be all right.' He had obviously noticed some tension in her.

She heard the striking of a match, the buzzing of a burner. 'I make coffee for you, Pippa.' His laugh came to her. 'No tea for English girl, sorry.'

Pippa relaxed and smiled at his figure hunched in the cabin doorway. She had been silly thinking such thoughts. She would welcome the coffee but was also beginning to feel hungry. He must have been feeling the same for he looked out at her. 'We eat later.' His eyes strayed to the boom above her. 'Be careful when you stand, Pippa. Not hit your head.'

She glanced up at it, watched it move a few inches from side to side against the azure sky, and wondered where they would eat later. Had he got some food on board, or would they go ashore?

They sat in the cockpit drinking their coffee, she on one side, he on the other. The sun was on her back, but the cool breeze off the sea made its heat pleasantly comfortable.

Tomas took his cap off, squinted across at her. 'Do you like my boat, Pippa?'

'I think it's lovely,' she answered truthfully, 'and I'm glad you brought me here. It's all so gorgeous — everything.' She saw the pleasure her words had obviously given him. He nodded. 'I'm pleased, pleased that you have come. You first woman to come on this boat.'

Pippa inclined her head graciously at the honour, and contented herself with saying, 'Thank you very much, I am enjoying every minute.' It sounded stilted, but it was better than getting tied up, perhaps in words that he would not understand, though actually his understanding of English was quite good, she was finding out. But conversation of any kind, intelligible, stilted or not with this man was delightful.

Tomas looked at her teasingly. 'Some say bad luck to have woman on boat,' his brown eyes glowed at her, 'I say good.'

Pippa made a mock grimace of fear, then laughed. 'I hope so.' Then she remembered the lack of a name on it. 'What is the name of the boat, Tomas?'

He stared at her a moment thoughtfully, serious faced. 'I not have a name for her.' His regard of her became more concentrated. 'Now I think I call her Filipa — like you. Very good do you think?'

'Well,' she hesitated, 'yes — it's very kind of you but . . . ' Pippa was stuck for words. What did one say when someone told you they were naming a boat after you? 'Are you sure — I mean, there must be lots of other names. I could — '

'No,' he interrupted, shaking his head and going on determinedly, 'I call her Filipa, I write it on,' he slapped the side of the boat, 'tomorrow.'

'I must say I've never had a boat named after me before, Tomas. It's quite an occasion.'

Tomas gazed at her in satisfaction, evidently greatly pleased with his decision, then he took the cup from her. 'I get more coffee. He stood up and shrugged apologetically, 'No wine, but maybe later.' He left her and bent into the cabin again.

Warning bells sounded in Pippa's mind. Wine — drink. Yes, for sure if she and Tomas were going to be each other's, but that was a dream with no possibility of it materialising. She sighed as he reappeared.

Handing her the cup, he said, 'We go for a sail soon,' he gestured sternwards, 'to Allemura.'

Pippa gazed up at him unable to keep her love out of her eyes. Nodded and smiled, happiness mixed with an ache from the knowledge that in two days' time they would part for ever.

7

Soon afterwards Tomas pulled up the anchor and began to unfurl the sails, first freeing the small one, then the larger, they accepting the breeze's invitation. Came the soft hiss as the boat began to move through the water, and Pippa watched as Tomas moved about with the easy relaxed tread of a man used to the sea and its ways. Then he seated himself at the stern on the same side as herself, hand resting lightly on the tiller, apparently allowing the boat to find its own way. He was as one with the craft. Eyes narrowed against the glare, a man appearing content and pleased.

Yet Pippa caught his glance at her occasionally — his reassuring smile then his eyes quickly away again. She got the feeling that he was working something out in his mind

— something regarding her. Found it rather strange that a man who earned his livelihood from the sea should still be attracted to it and sail upon it for the pleasure it gave him.

She gazed past the towering sail, spray lightly damping her face, the thought occurring that anyone married to a man like Tomas might come second to his boat. But better that than to another woman. She sighed. It could never be for her.

To her right Pippa saw they were passing Fisherman's beach — the one they had just crossed to reach the boat. Just ahead she could see the golden tip of Allemura beach separated from the former by large towering rocks. At low tide one could be reached from the other.

Some quarter of an hour later Tomas hove the boat to and anchored immediately off Allemura. Pippa could see the white lines of waves foaming on to the shore. Strange she thought, to see them from behind — to watch them begin from nothing then gain momentum and size. Directly in front of her was the tunnel running from the beach to the town centre, and to its immediate right she saw the commanding oblong of the Algarve hotel and its terrace with umbrellas.

She turned to find Tomas standing looking down at her, balancing easily to the slow roll of the boat. He pointed shorewards. 'We go have something to eat, Pippa. You hungry?'

'I certainly am,' she replied with feeling. 'I could eat a man off his horse.' She saw him mouthing the words in an attempt to understand, and laughed. 'Don't worry, Tomas, it's just an old English saying.'

He shrugged, but amusement lurked in his eyes. 'England is full of strange words. I think. We go and eat something much better than man on horse, eh?'

He leaned over the stern and brought the dinghy alongside, then helped her into it, she making a more graceful entry than when leaving it earlier to board the boat.

They arrived amongst the bathers, the dinghy riding on the waves at an alarmingly fast rate for the last few yards. His hand covered hers as she helped him pull the small boat ashore, Tomas getting his trousers wet and she the hem of her skirt. It didn't matter, the sun would dry them in minutes. They strolled hand in hand up the beach towards the steps leading to the hotel terrace. Pippa saw the women eyeing Tomas, lifting their heads to gaze after him. She felt proud at his side.

The terrace was very busy — the far end filled with hotel residents on sun loungers — and where Pippa and Tomas were, people were eating and drinking under the umbrellas. There was just one table empty by the wall overlooking the beach. Tomas led her to it and Pippa saw that it had four chairs and hoped fervently that nobody else would join them.

They both decided on a fish salad and Tomas went off to fetch it from the self-service at the rear of the terrace. There he turned and waved through the large window and she lifted her hand in reply.

Five minutes later he returned with the salads, also a bottle of wine and glasses. He filled her glass then his own, smiled into her face. 'We drink to Pippa and Tomas,' he said clinking his glass against hers with a flourish.

She repeated the toast, eyes meeting his above the glasses. The wine was white and fairly sweet — the bottle blue green with a quaint English sounding name — Lancers on the label.

He must have noticed her glance at it. 'All right, not strong,' he assured her. She brought her chair nearer to the table, her back to the others on the terrace as if to keep the rest of the world away. Glanced at Tomas, busy savaging the virgin array on his plate. He was hers perhaps, for the next forty-eight hours, then would come the void, an aching heart for years afterwards. And he? Maybe he would remember her occasionally by the name on the boat, that was if he really meant to name it after her.

She became aware that he was addressing her, pointing to her plate. 'You like it?' She came out of her thoughts quickly. Nodded enthusiastically. 'Thank you.' It was sardines and shell fish served with rice on crisp lettuce, and firm slices of tomato and onion. The latter she had not touched yet. She smiled wryly to herself. Would he kiss her before the day was out? He had made no pass at her so far. She bent her head to her plate again. Was it perhaps that he didn't care enough, seeing her only as a companion for the afternoon? She sighed inwardly. This man made her moods change rapidly, hot and cold, up and down. Happy, then sad.

Pippa glanced up at Tomas to find him pulling his pullover off. She'd wondered earlier how he could stick it — he must be boiled, although on the boat there had been a cool breeze. She observed him over her glass discreetly. His shirt had become unbuttoned to the waist, its edges pulled apart. She was reminded of the statues of Roman athletes — one in particular in an encyclopaedia once given to her by her parents, a picture in it of a man wrestling with a python. His chest sculptured in muscle. No flaccid flesh as on some of the male holidaymakers she had seen.

She realised that she was staring at him and that he was smiling back with a tolerant amusement. He must think she was a dreamer, it being the second time she had drifted away in thought.

'You were thinking?' he asked gently.

Had her gaze betrayed her thoughts? 'I — I was just thinking how beautiful it is here. I shall remember this as my favourite place.'

'Portugal?'

She nodded, looking around, avoiding his probing dark eyes. 'Well, this part — I haven't seen any more of the country.'

'Why do you like it so much, Pippa?'

'Oh, the colours, it's bright, cheerful, sunny. People enjoying themselves.'

Tomas's smile remained, but his brow had furrowed. 'Not always like this, Pippa. You see people on holiday like you.' A sadness rested on his features, 'not Portuguese, they work.'

'But surely they get holidays sometimes?'

'Ye-e-s,' he replied slowly, 'but not long holidays, they are not paid very well.'

She understood but was still puzzled. 'What about all the tourists? They bring money into the country.'

Tomas looked doubtful. 'That is true, Pippa, but not all Portuguese work at tourists.'

Pippa smiled at his occasionally confused English. 'I know what you mean.'

Tomas smiled wryly at her. 'I like tourists coming here . . . ' he shrugged, 'but then sometimes not.' Seeing the question in her face, he continued, 'Once I go to Spain. I see big buildings, high buildings. They build for tourists, spoil the country. Bad for Portugal. I do not want to see that. Better that tourists not come.'

Pippa smiled at him in comforting agreement. 'But I'm sure they will not let that happen here, Tomas. The authorities will have learned a lesson from what's happened in Spain.'

Suddenly Tomas's expression changed. His eyes danced to hers. 'Heh. I talk miserable — no good. It is no good for you, Pippa.' He picked up the bottle, refilled her glass before she could refuse, filled his own. 'You drink to Filipa. I paint the name tomorrow.'

Pippa laughed with pleasure. 'Good idea. I'm honoured.' She must be careful not to have any more wine. It was too easy to drink.

They pointed their glasses at the boat, its cabin and furled sails sandwiched sharply white between the blue of sea and sky. 'To Filipa,' they chorused, and the people nearby looked on curiously.

It was wonderful under the umbrella in the company of Tomas, and she did not want it to end ever. Talking of the boat's name reminded her that she did not know her companion's surname. He had never mentioned it. She watched as he drank, then placed his glass on the table between them.

'Tomas, what is your surname — your last name? You know mine — Gentle. What is yours?' She saw the quick, guarded look appear to vanish almost immediately, making her think it had never been there at all. She waited expectantly.

Tomas's shoulders moved upward slightly. Waved a dismissive hand. 'It is not important. I like you to call me Tomas all the time.'

'Oh, I will,' Pippa replied readily, 'but you know mine; I just wanted to know yours, that's all.' She smiled. 'Do you think I would not be able to pronounce it? See if I can,' she persisted.

134

He hesitated momentarily. 'Da Silva.'
'Da Silva,' she repeated after him.
Tomas Da Silva. It had quite a ring
with it. She observed him as he picked
up his glass again. The way he held it.
That glass was not expensive, but his
fingers, and the way he did hold it
spoke of more expensive things. A man
of some mystery. A fisherman, yet with
no roughness about him, and Pippa had
the feeling that he was better educated
than most of those she had seen. His
English, whilst not perfect, was good. In
fact she had noticed occasionally his
use of words that only a person well
versed in English conversation would
have used. She drained her own glass to
hide her thoughts from him, then sat
back in her chair, changed the subject.
'Thank you very much for the meal
Tomas. I've enjoyed it.' She sighed
heavily. 'In the winter I shall try and
cheer myself up by thinking and
remembering this glorious day —
your boat and this terrace, it's been
heavenly.'

Tomas shot her a peculiar look before turning in his chair to look out over the beach. Did she glimpse sadness, something akin to fear? Or had she just imagined it? He glanced back at her, and if it had been there, it had now gone, his eyes twinkling brown at her.

'You would like coffee on boat, Pippa,' he enquired, 'or I get coffee here?' He half rose.

'No — no, Tomas.' She put out a hand. 'I'd love it on the boat, I'm sure.'

He looked pleased, and they got up to leave, Pippa glancing back to the table and its umbrella. An oasis holding a pleasant memory, but tinged with a sadness of her own.

Whilst Tomas rowed her back to the boat Pippa day-dreamed. Da Silva. If she were married to him it would be Mrs. Da Silva. No, that was wrong. Senhora Da Silva, Senhora Pippa Da Silva. It sounded good, his wife. If only . . . She sighed deeply, inwardly. Life was full of obstacles, and ifs.

She looked at the object of her

thoughts, as he glanced over his shoulder, keeping the dinghy in line with the boat. He had not spoken since leaving the beach. And again she saw the preoccupied expression. What was he thinking about? His shirt had become damp with perspiration, making the material cling to his body, emphasising the taper from the shoulders to the slim waist. She wondered why he had been reluctant to divulge his surname. It couldn't possibly make any difference to her whatever his name had been. Was Da Silva his real name? He had hesitated before telling her.

On board again she sat with her back to the cabin, head resting against its warm wood. To her left she could see the terrace they had just left — the very table they had sat at now occupied by someone else. To her right a motor boat sped towards the horizon, its wash just beginning to roll Tomas's boat gently.

Pippa closed her eyes, feeling pleasantly drowsy. It must be the effect of the wine, she thought. Should have stuck to a lemonade, or some such drink. Just behind her head, she could hear Tomas busy in the cabin.

Perhaps it was his shadow hiding the sun, or the cessation of sounds from the cabin that made her open her eyes again.

He was stood above her, tall to the sky, matching the mast and gazing down on her. She sat up. 'I must have dozed off.'

He smiled at her, handed her the cup. But she had glimpsed the intense desire in his eyes before the masking smile was born. A shaft of apprehension went through her. Had she been wise returning to the boat with him? But it was too late for misgivings, and anyway why did she keep trying to delude herself? This was what she had wished for dearly ever since she had met him. To be completely alone with him, and let things take their course.

Tomas settled himself opposite her, one leg resting along the seat, and regarded her sideways. 'You have enjoyed your sail, Pippa?'

'Very much, Tomas. I'm glad you asked me to come,' she replied appreciatively. 'Your boat is beautiful and you see,' she smiled at him, 'I haven't been sick at all. Are you ever sea sick?'

'No, I am used to it, much practice sailing.' There was a gleam of amusement as he turned to look straight at her. 'It is good that we be together, Pippa,' to which she silently and fervently agreed.

From behind her came the muted roar of the waves upon the beach, and nearer the gentle slap of the water against the boat sides. It occurred to her that if she were to take back home a memory of this man it must be as full a one as possible so that in years to come she could relive it — however sad the memory. She must find out more about him.

'How long have you been a fisherman, Tomas?'

Tomas contemplated something in the distance for a few moments before replying briefly, 'long time.'

'D'you like it?' Saw his slight grimace.

'It is work,' he stated simply. He turned to her. 'I'm old fisherman now.' His face was perfectly straight but she observed the twitch upwards of his mouth corners.

'You're certainly not,' Pippa laughed dismissively at this. 'You're no more than I am — twenty-three, nearly,' she informed him.

'Ah,' he exclaimed with a stern satisfaction, 'then I am old — I am vinte e cinco — twenty-five.' His lips began to widen.

Two years older than herself. 'What month were you born, Tomas?'

'Julho — July.'

'No wonder you're a fisherman. You were born under the water sign — Cancer the crab. Mine's November,' she volunteered.

'Novembro — this month?'

'Yes, the twenty-seventh, two days after I get back,' she said regretfully. Shrugged mentally. No doubt she'd celebrate it by herself or with a couple of friends quietly.

Tomas's face had become thoughtful. 'Vinte e sete,' he muttered as if to himself.

'I'll be back in grey old England,' she sighed. 'I shall think of you, Tomas.'

Think of him! Her mind would be full of nothing else for years to come. Suddenly she remembered the camera in her bag. She would take a shot of him. She found it and brought it out with a flourish. 'I'm going to take a photo of you, Tomas.' She put it to her eye, but he waved a hand in front of it, a deep frown upon his face, and Pippa was surprised until she saw the humour in the mouth and eyes.

'No,' he said firmly, 'I photograph you, you have the beauty.'

It was her turn to demur. 'I shall take the first snap, it is a woman's privilege, an old English custom.' She saw his face crease as he chuckled his disbelief. Moving away towards the stern she hunched behind the lens, seeing Tomas sat against the cabin bulkhead.

He looked stern and proud and perhaps a little formal as she looked at him. Her heart tried to shout to him through the camera. 'Love me, Tomas, tell me you love me. Just something to remember you by. Not a flat coloured picture. Please — please.' She pressed the shutter. 'There, a perfect one. You look very handsome.' How many more girls had his picture on their bedroom walls? she wondered.

'Now I take you.' He grasped the camera eagerly, and Pippa went and sat against the cabin bulkhead as he had done. Her pose was unnatural she felt, and a brittle smile upon her face to mask the pain in her heart, but it would not hide her feelings. They would show plainly, she was sure.

The shutter clicked, and Tomas gave a sigh of satisfaction. 'Most pretty picture. Very good.' He looked thoughtful but to Pippa's regret did not say he wanted a copy.

He stood easily to the boat's rolling in the stern and then surprised her by saying, 'together now, Pippa, we have photograph.'

'Wish we could. I'd love one of us together. But there's no one else to take us.' An idea came. 'I know, we can ask someone to take us when we get on the beach, I'm sure . . . ' She stopped. Tomas was shaking his head and motioning her to join him.

'Come here, Pippa,' he commanded, 'I show you how. Do it here.'

Puzzled as to how he was going to manage it she went towards him holding on to the boom to steady herself. Tomas seated her in the stern, then positioned himself beside her and stretched his arm out in front of him with the camera pointed towards themselves. He threw a smile at her, evidently pleased with his solution to the problem. The camera was small in his palm, his thumb hovering over the button. When he spoke his voice was low, thick. 'We must be close together, then the photograph all right.'

He brought his head nearer to hers, their hair touching, his arm curving around her waist, his hand warm through her dress below her breast. His nearness and maleness were an assault upon her senses. She had no defence — her heart had been stolen long ago.

His thumb moved upon the camera casing. Momentarily Pippa's imagination ran riot. She and Tomas leaning over the wedding cake, the photographer taking a shot of them close together. 'Just one more.' The laughter and good wishes, married from home.

Tomas was talking. 'I take another, perhaps that one no good.'

She nodded, took it from him and wound it on — the number in the little window showing one more left. Returned it, patted her hair and settled with her head close to his again.

The picture taken, Tomas moved his

head away, turned to her. 'Now we have two pictures, one for me, one for you.'

Pippa looked up at him from the crook of his arm still about her. Could feel the strong firm pad of chest muscle against her. He had said 'we'. How wonderful it sounded, and yet his one for her and one for him seemed to signify their parting for ever in some two days' time, each with a photograph of the other.

Strangely the sea had gone quiet, Tomas's eyes dark caves, blotting out the sky. She felt his lips settle lightly to brush along hers, his hand etching a butterfly line down her cheek. In an involuntary gesture her fingers flew to her lips as if to hold in his kiss for always. She wanted to arch her body bow-like against his, arms fast about him, ploughing her fingers through the dark strong hair at the nape of his neck.

In reality she took the camera from him with an unsteady hand and put it into her bag. What it contained was very precious. She knew that if she tried to stand up now, she would fall, her legs were so weak. Tremulously, she asked without looking at him, 'D'you think the photographs will be ready tomorrow if I take them to the shop today?' Her inner being mocked her. One kiss and she was shying away like a nervous filly.

She glanced up to see the heaviness in his eyes fading and an awakening comprehension taking its place. He looked across the water frowning. Her question had obviously started him thinking. She guessed that he had forgotten for the moment that she was leaving on Saturday.

'Saturday?' he questioned, maintaining his gaze over the water, his fingers restless against her waist.

She sighed. 'Yes, I leave all this,' adding silently, and you. Went on reflectively, speaking at his profile, 'Do you know that when you asked me to come for a sail it crossed my mind that you might try to kidnap me again.'

Tomas turned to her, his face grown

intently serious. Had she offended him? Perhaps she should not have said that. It must be the wine — she had been foolish to have more than one glass. She began to apologise, 'that was silly of me, I sh . . . '

'No,' he interrupted forcefully, 'what you say is true.' His eyes held hers, fierce challenging desire in them. 'I want to kidnap you again for always.'

She stared at him as if hypnotised. 'W — what do you mean?' she said unsteadily, breathlessly. Her brain was trying to tell her something.

His grip tightened around her waist, his other hand finding and clasping hers strongly, so that she winced. 'Stay here, Pippa, stay with me — don't go home,' he beseeched her. 'I want you. You live here with me, in Allemura. That is why I wanted to keep you at the apartment until your plane had gone. Not for money — only so I could ask you.' His eyes glowed. 'We marry. I look after you. I make you happy.'

'Marry!' The word was wrenched

from her, a disbelieving stupified sound.

He must have misunderstood her exclamation. 'But you say you love me once — remember.' His eyes were brown diamonds boring into hers. 'Today I ask you on the beach you say you meant it.'

'Oh, I do — I do, Tomas, never will you know how much, it's just that I have to think.' How? Her mind was a glorious confusion. He had asked her to stay and marry him. Her mind for the moment refused to work further.

With an easy strength Tomas twisted her round until her upper body was against his. Her face resting in the hairy jungle of his chest, and feeling the beat of his heart beneath. His passionate kisses covered her head like rain drops, then touching her ears and hovering teasingly round her mouth. His fingers stroked the rounded sides of her throat.

She was trembling, her hands finding their way beneath his shirt, feeling the muscular ridges of his back. He muttered her name between the caresses of his lips and words in his own language. She did not understand, cared nothing, gasping in a sweet agony of torture.

Tomas's mouth came down on hers thrusting her lips aside brutally, crushing them ravenously. His hands found the back of her legs and he lifted her into his arms. With sure steps against the boat's movement he carried Pippa to the cabin entrance. Then, still supporting her, he set her down — she would have fallen otherwise. Guided her to the bunk and eased her down upon it. It was cool and shaded, and very private in there. Then leaning over her his lips descended passionately upon hers again, stroking her own highly charged emotions further.

Her hands stroked his head, feeling the crisp full hair, her fingers arching and furrowing through it as his lips found her throat. Gasped as he found the softness at its base. A faint voice deep in her joy kept repeating, He wants to marry you. She must hear him say it again, make sure. 'D'you really want to marry me, Tomas?' she murmured. The pressure of his lips eased from her throat, his voice seemed far away.

'Sim, yes.'

'Say it to me again, Tomas please.'

The weight of his upper body moved. 'I tell you, I want to marry you, Pippa.'

Through the haze of her happiness did she discern a note of irritation? she opened her eyes.

He raised himself, leaning on an arm, looked down on her. 'You not believe I want to marry you, Pippa?'

She reached up, caressed his face with her fingers. 'Of course I believe you. It's just that I wanted to hear you say it again ... God, I've prayed a million times these last days that you would ask me. Now I can't believe that it's true — that it's actually happened to me. I love you so much.'

She gave a shuddering sigh. 'Oh, so

much.' Took his hand, kissed each finger in turn.

His eyes darkened with a quick return of passion, yet his voice held a note of bitter humour as he pointed down at her. 'You ask me to tell you again, but you do not tell me that you will marry me.'

'I know, Tomas, but you've taken me by surprise — a marvellous, beautiful surprise.' She kissed his hand again on its brown back, clung to it. 'You see, I never really believed that it would come to me, the thing I wanted most in my life. Now it's happened, and I can't think straight.'

With an effort she sat up, her legs over the wide end of the bunk, glad of the respite for the fast crumbling defences of her body. Tomas would not have been a man if he had not tried. But she knew that if he took her fully in his arms again she could not resist him. Nothing would matter then but the sweet powerful touch of his lips atop of hers. She would not care whether

Tomas felt passionate hard desire for her or a true love.

Slowly, reluctantly, Tomas raised himself alongside her, put an arm around her shoulders in a protective tender gesture. 'You strange English girl, Pippa. You are most beautiful woman. Always I want to marry you — any man would.'

Impulsively she turned and kissed him hard on the cheek, her expression baring her soul to him. Happiness upon happiness. Suddenly she felt dizzy, perhaps she would feel better in the fresh air outside the cabin.

She passed a hand across her face. 'Could we sit outside, Tomas? I feel a little faint. I think it's the wine and the warmth in here.'

Tomas looked concerned, uttered a sound of annoyance at himself. 'Desculpe — sorry. I do not think.' A deep frown formed and stayed, but beneath it she discerned the gleam. 'You will not marry a man who does not think.'

He guided her carefully, his arms around her, to the seat outside, where Pippa took a deep breath and leaned her head back against the bulkhead. 'A few minutes, and I shall be all right, Tomas.'

He stood looking down at her anxiously. 'I get you coffee — presto — black.'

'No, no, don't bother, but thank you.'

He sat down beside her, staring at her, his expression urgent and expectant. Above them, the halyards tinkled against the mast, and the boom swung a little more in the cooling late afternoon breeze. 'Your plane goes tomorrow, Pippa?'

She nodded, her eyes resting on his, her mind still recovering from the shock of his offer of marriage.

'If you go, you never come back to me. I know that.' His eyes probed hers, seeking a denial of his statement.

'Oh, yes, I would, Tomas,' she

asserted earnestly, 'I would. Nothing would stop me. I — I love you.'

He clutched her to him closely bending her backwards, his face above her, suddenly commanding, imperious. 'When, Pippa, when will you say you marry me?'

Pippa's mind raced. She knew what her answer was going to be — there was never any doubt as to that, but she needed time to think — about her mother's future and other things. She kissed him full and hard on the lips, then drew her mouth away sharply, pushing gently against his chest. Had decided what she was going to do. With eyes shining, she exclaimed, 'Sail me round to the Praia-da-Oura! Then . . .' She stumbled hesitantly over the foreign words. That beach meant a great deal to her.

'Then you tell me?' he asked eagerly, huskily.

She nodded, her eyes dancing wickedly at him. 'Yes or no.'

'You better say yes, then I can teach

you to speak Portuguese.' His lips smiled but his fear of rejection registered fleetingly.

Pippa glimpsed it. He really did want to marry her.

8

Pippa watched him as he began to make preparations to move on to Priaia-da-Oura beach. How could she think of life without him now? She relaxed as they began to gather way, fingers trailing in the passing water — the latter caressing her fingers as lightly as his kisses had touched her eyes. But his mouth in the cabin had been devouring, brutal, aggressive. Making her all but powerless under the spell he had cast over her.

Unseeingly she gazed at the shoreline drifting by, her heartbeats matching the dancing sparklers upon the water. Still stunned that fate should have taken her hand and given to her her heart's desire.

They sailed on, Pippa occasionally catching Tomas's eye. He would smile, his glance lingering on her, both conscious of the great secret they shared of being in love. He would then look away again regretfully in order to keep them on course. The freshening breeze heeled the boat more, making it slice through the waves and pick up speed as if it were conscious of the impatient urgency of its helmsman.

Pippa's thoughts ran on, but under her sky of delirious joy a cloud of reasoning and questioning began to form. He wanted to marry her, that was true. But was he doing it out of pity for her, the right thing? Did he really love her? He had shown desire, but he had never mentioned love, that he loved her. Could she trust him? Had love for her overtaken and overwhelmed him so quickly as it had herself?

And what arrangements could she make for her mother? She couldn't just marry Tomas and leave her mother to fend for herself. There was John, her brother. Would he be willing to take their mother in to live permanently with him in the South of England? In any case she, Pippa, would have to go home. She couldn't just send a telegram to say that she had accepted a proposal of marriage from a Portuguese, and leave it at that. She had dreamed of marriage to Tomas and her love for him had filled her mind. Now the problems associated with such a marriage were showing themselves.

Pippa shrugged mentally. Other people of different nationalities had married — they would have had the same problems, and no doubt had got over them. After all it was her life and some way would be found to take care of her mother. It was bound though to come as a shock to her and to the family.

She became aware that they were coming abreast of Priaia-da-Oura beach. Noted the rock she had sat against and fallen asleep. That day when she had tried to steal away before Tomas could see her. She shuddered inwardly at the thought that she would never have known the happiness now flooding her whole being if she had succeeded.

People were still bathing and others sat up on the terrace. Behind, the apartments rose dazzling white. But it was the line of small boats drawn up on the sand that caught and held Pippa's gaze. Like coloured fish laid out to dry. That row of boats held a very special place in her mind, and one craft in particular. She recognised it, fresh and brightly coloured. Paint that he had been putting on when she had conversed with him for the first time. Now by a miracle Tomas was with her and waiting for her answer to his proposal of marriage.

She glanced at him to find his eyes fixed on her, a dark, deep longing in them. She wanted to keep the memory of it in her mind's eye for ever, to reassure herself that it had been there — not just desire but the look of love alongside. The look faded as he smiled and nodded at the shore, 'Praia-da-Oura,' then adjusted the sheets and the boat began to slow.

A few minutes later they were just drifting, the sails down and crumpled. Tomas turned to Pippa, his regard of her now unyielding, searching into her face for her answer.

She glanced away over the now small white rollers to his fishing boat on the sand. 'Take me to the beach, Tomas, please.' Saw his surprise and hesitation.

'Praia-da-Oura?'

'Is it too dangerous?'

He gave the shoreline a swift appraisal, and shook his head. 'No, might get wet a little.' He turned to her, forehead lines deepened in puzzlement.

'I'd love you for ever if you will.' Her words were spoken lightly, but her face and manner were extremely serious, the blue eyes intently solemn. Evidently enough to convince him that it was most important to her to set foot on that beach. He nodded as if something had just occurred to him. His lips stretched in a smile of understanding. His hand caressed her cheek as he got

160

up and went forward, then dropped the anchor overboard.

The dinghy was borne shoreward by the waves. In a matter of minutes it was sliding along the sandy bottom and Tomas jumped out and handed Pippa through the foaming water on to the beach before dragging the dinghy clear.

Pippa ran up ahead of him towards the line of fishing boats. She had had to come back to that particular beach. High excitement was in her, emotions beginning to erupt in her heart and making her tremble. She made for Tomas's boat, colourful in its blue, white and green. Put her hand upon it — it meant a great deal to her. It had been instrumental in bringing them together. He had been attending to it when she had first seen him. It was a symbol to her of their love, and so, too, was the other boat in which he had just asked her to marry him.

She stood waiting, proud and bursting with love for Tomas as he walked towards her, his trousers moulded by the breeze against the muscular shape of his thighs. Wanting to make those few minutes last and last. To stay young, have that moment forever. Instinctively she knew that she was approaching the most powerful moments in a woman's life. A queen holding sway over her subject.

Tomas stared at her with hot and questioning eyes. He was breathing quickly, not all from the exertion of pulling the dinghy up the sand. Seeing her heaving breasts, the blue eyes which outshone the sky in their deep emotion.

For Pippa all and everything had disappeared, the terrace, people, noises. Only she and Tomas remained between two fishing boats on a small island of love. Her words came breathlessly, soft against the sea breeze. 'Now, Tomas my love, ask me to marry you.' She saw the swift realisation in his eyes, then the dissolving of his normally serious cast into an uncontainable joy. Words rushed at her in Portuguese. She shook her head, controlled herself just long enough to utter, 'in English, dear love. Say it to me.' A delirious and glorious moment. Saw his great effort. Like a bow stretched to its limit.

'Pippa, Pippa. Marry me, por favor — '

Tears glistened through her deep emotions. 'Yes, oh yes Tomas, I will,' she gasped ecstatically.

The next moment she was swung off her feet into his arms. Then he danced in great circles down the beach, round and round until she felt dizzy, his bursting ecstasy matching her own, and finding release in the joyous action. They reached the water and he stopped at its edge, still carrying her. He brought her head up to his mouth, kissed her savagely, greedily.

How long the kiss lasted neither of them knew nor cared. When it was over he continued to carry her along the water's edge, stopping occasionally to gaze down at her, then out to the sea. He was like some primeval man showing off his mate. The fisherman bringing his bride-to-be for the sea's approval. Then he put her down, and she staggered unsteadily, drunk from his kisses. He caught her to him and she arched and moulded against his hard bodied maleness. Tomas murmuring things she did not understand.

Perhaps it was the sound of children's voices close by, the splash of water upon her that brought Pippa from heaven to earth again. Opening her eyes, she glanced down reluctantly. An orange coloured beach ball was floating away on the retreating waves and two charging children plunging through the water towards it. Their loves would come later.

The interruption gave her the chance to find her tongue. 'I had to come back to this beach, Tomas. It was where I first met you, that was why I asked you to bring me here again.' She felt his heart beating powerfully against her.

His voice vibrated through her. 'I see you pass me every day. I think you the most beautiful woman in the world.'

Pippa sighed in pure pleasure, in sheer happiness. 'I prayed that something would happen to make you notice me. I think I loved you before I'd even spoken to you.' She lifted her face up to him again. 'I love you, Tomas.' She pouted her lips, closed her eyes to receive him again.

Instead he spoke with a note of sadness. 'I love you then but I did not know if you love me. In the apartment that day you were angry with me. I know I love you,' he sighed heavily, 'But I thought you hate me. Then the building fall. I think you die — I die, not live without you.'

She looked up at him. 'Oh, Tomas, I'm glad you did kidnap me.'

'So am I now.' He smiled down at her in tenderness and desire. Then he glanced up toward the terrace. 'We shall go to the café. We have drink and celebrate.'

Arms around each other, they began a more sober retracing of their steps up the beach. She observed her own footprints of a short time ago when she had run on ahead of him to stand by the fishing boat. Those marks in the sand belonged to a world away, before she had agreed to marry him. She could feel his excitement and loving energy passing into her through their tightly clasped hands.

Tomas nodded at the boat when they were nearly abreast of it, his eyes dancing at her. 'I paint that very badly.'

She looked at him in some surprise. 'I think it's gorgeous, such beautiful colours, and it shines. But why d'you say that?'

Deep humour glinted from him. 'Each day I was busy looking for you. I look for you and not at the boat. I do not paint straight.'

And Pippa giggled lovingly up at him.

The terrace, even so late in the afternoon, was still busy, and a contrast flashed through Pippa's mind. Those terrace seats were not long unoccupied throughout the day. At home the seats in the park would already be empty, forlorn and forgotten until the next spring.

Pippa began to feel self-conscious as they made towards the rear of the terrace. Had their unbridled kisses been observed? Certainly Tomas's circular progress to the water with her in his arms must have been. Tomas led her by the hand across the narrow courtyard into the small bar-cum-café beyond, where a few people were sitting at the tables. Pippa had been in there once before.

With an obvious pride and happiness Tomas introduced her to the two young men behind the counter, and to the girl at the cash till near the exit. Then followed a short explanatory conversation between Tomas and the others, and an even briefer one-sided conversation between the assistants and Pippa which Tomas translated as congratulations being offered her.

Before they sat down Pippa excused herself and went to the ladies' room. As she dried her hands she gazed at herself in the mirror. Flushed, bright eyes, almost feverishly so. Wild haired, but her heart beating jubilantly, joyously. Could it be true? Or was she dozing on her hotel bed to wake up soon?

She convinced herself that this was reality. There was no turning back now. Her prayer had been answered. She was to marry Tomas da Silva, the fisherman from Priaia-da-Oura beach. He had said he loved her, and she with all her heart loved him. A tiny regret came, that there was no one she knew to whom she could rush and call out her happiness and great news. She was alone in a foreign land.

Back in the café she found Tomas waiting for her at a table at one end of the room. She slid along the soft smooth length of its seat and was glad it was a little more private than some of the tables, but then she was sure that Tomas was a private sort of person. There was an intense desire in the hard muscular pressure of his thigh against hers, and also in the glowing brown eyes that he now turned upon her.

She saw that there were two glasses of water coloured liquid as well as sandwiches and coffee. High emotion and excitement had taken her appetite away and also it was not long since she had eaten on the terrace at Allemura. Tomas pushed one of the glasses towards her, then waved a hand towards the counter. 'They want to give bottle of wine for us, but I tell them about your head . . . ' He described expressive circles with his hand. 'So I think you like this instead.'

Pippa looked up at him. 'It was very kind of them, Tomas, but I'm glad you refused the wine. I don't think I could take any more.' She raised her glass, sniffed its contents. 'What is this?'

'S'all right, not bad for you. Only small glass.'

She glanced up to find the two young men and the girl watching her, so raised her glass in acknowledgement of their salutations, then took a small amount.

It was awful. She subdued a grimace, aware of Tomas's gaze.

Then they touched glasses in a toast to each other. 'Saude,' said Tomas. 'To my wife of the future.'

Pippa smiled in great joy, her heart beating faster at the thought. 'S — saude. To my future husband.' It was as in a dream saying and hearing such things. She was glad however that he had made no attempt to kiss or hold her in front of the other people present in the café. Away from there it would be different.

They made a start on the refreshments, Pippa drinking the coffee and taking occasional sips of the white liquid. Each silently delighting in the new company of the other. This was how it would be she thought, man and wife sat together side by side. In their house. She wondered where they would live; somewhere near Allemura, no doubt. And when would they get married? Thoughts of the marriage prompted another.

She put her small fair hand upon his large brown one. 'I shall have to go home first, Tomas,' she said gently, 'to make some arrangements for mother.'

The happiness in his eyes faded. 'I want you to stay here, Pippa. Better . . . ' He paused thoughtfully. 'I remember you have brother.'

'Yes, I have, Tomas, but he lives a long way away from here. He also has a family and it would be difficult to take her to live with him immediately. Anyway, she may not want to go and live with him, and she's not a well person at all.' Pippa sighed. 'It's not as simple as that.' Suddenly a marvellous idea came. She grasped his arm with a renewed excitement, enthusiasm. 'Why don't you come home with me, Tomas?' It would be good to show her new-found love off to her family and friends.

'It is not possible, Pippa.' He shrugged. 'Some day perhaps, but I have to work here, I need to work, then we can marry.'

His eyes enveloped her, a troubled humour in them. 'We just meet, now already you going to leave me. It will be a long time.'

'Perhaps a week or so, Tomas my love.'

He nodded at her sombrely. 'That is a long time to me.'

Pippa gazed at him. How she loved him and wanted to mould into his arms. Instead she reached out and fingered the strong coarse hair, saw the passion flare in his eyes again. His hand tightened on hers and she caught the curious, wondering stares of others.

She finished her coffee, then looked into the liquid remaining in her glass. Suddenly she was fearful of herself. If she returned home would the magic of Tomas and the place where she had found him be lost? Would she realise the impracticability of her venture? See it for what it was — a romantic, impossible dream to perish in the dim light of the northern mists?

And while she was away would he

begin to regret his proposal to her? Would he still be waiting for her when she returned? That girl Carmella was no doubt still around. Another thought came — perhaps they could marry and live in England. But inwardly, Pippa guessed not. There was very little work to be had at that time. In any case, Tomas was a fisherman — a man of the sea and of the sun. In Halford the former was conspicuously absent and the latter almost so.

'Are you having doubts already?' His deep accented teasing tones at her ear startled her from her thoughts.

She turned quickly, smilingly, hugged his arm with both hands. 'Of course not. I'm sorry, I was just thinking. Rude of me.'

His eyes studied her closely. 'Can I guess? You worry about your mother, huh?'

Pippa nodded, pursed her lips wistfully. 'A little, but not really worried, Tomas. But I am so happy I want them all — all my family — to be here with me just now. To see you — us. I still can't believe what has happened to me today.'

'Then we are both alike, Pippa. I am the same.' His eyes grew dark and she felt his passion flowing like a tangible thing over her, saw him make a notable effort to control himself and glance around as if becoming aware that they were still in the café. 'You like family very much Pippa, I think,' he stated, then went on, 'perhaps we shall have a family.' She saw the growing mischievous gleam. 'Make one quickly. We go back to boat now.'

She laughed, squeezed his hand lovingly, conscious of the effect his nearness and words were having on her.

His expression changed, became serious, thoughtful. 'One day, perhaps you bring your mother to Portugal to live.'

'Oh, that would be marvellous, Tomas,' Pippa exclaimed, but then wondered doubtfully whether her mother would want to reside there permanently, leaving John and his family over in England. All the same, it was kind of Tomas to think of that.

Suddenly she wanted to be outside again, away from thoughts and talk about her mother. This had been the most exciting day of her life. A very special day — hers and Tomas's. She felt an overwhelming and selfish desire to think only of herself and the man by her side for the remainder of that day at least.

She emptied her glass, put it firmly down upon the table. Saw that he also had finished. 'Shall we go now, Tomas?' she suggested.

He smiled in agreement. 'Of course,' then indicated her glass. 'Did you like that?'

'Yes, I did, that was just enough wine for me otherwise I should have been falling asleep.'

'It was a very special brandy — not a wine,' he said regarding her with a smiling tolerance as he would a child.

'From the Arbutus — strawberry tree,' he added.

'You know a lot about wine and such, Tomas. You seem to,' she said directly, and was surprised to see the fleeting guarded expression.

'Portugal is the land of wines, but we make other things, too,' he informed her with some pride.

Pippa was further surprised to realise that Tomas's English, whilst always passable, had become suddenly much better.

He rose from his seat, and she started to do the same, but he pressed her back gently. 'One moment, Pippa.'

Pippa saw him speak briefly to one of the Portuguese assistants who bent down behind the counter for a few moments, then handed something to him. When Tomas returned to their table, Pippa was surprised to see that he had a piece of cardboard about a foot square. He sat down again and smoothed the cardboard flat with his hands. 'Have you pen, Pippa?' he asked.

'A pen? What d'you want a pen for?' She looked at him in puzzled amusement.

Tomas did not answer but just smiled mysteriously.

She took her bag and searched its pockets. Found the pen she had used to write home. She handed it to him, watching in deepening puzzlement as he began in a purposeful manner to write something in large capital letters on the cardboard.

Bending closely over his hand she saw the letters take shape, but could not understand the words they made, presuming them to be Portuguese. When two lines had been completed he started again beneath them in smaller letters, and Pippa saw his name being formed, then numbers after it. 'Now it is done,' he said, gazing at his handiwork at arm's length.

There was a satisfaction in his profile, and yet Pippa caught a note of regret. She could not contain her curiosity any longer. 'Tomas, please tell me, what have you written? What's it for?'

'I sell the boat,' he proclaimed, leaning back in his seat and regarding her. 'I shall put this on the boat, people will see it, they stop, they buy.' He nodded at her. 'I know some who have asked me about it. I shall put it on the beach out of water, soon sell.'

Pippa stared at him, astonished. 'Why, Tomas? It's yours and it's beautiful. You love it, I know. Why d'you want to sell it now?' She knew what the boat meant to him. Had seen the pride and care with which he had handled it.

He leaned towards her, grasped her hands in his. 'I have something more important than boat to look after now. You!'

At that moment Pippa wanted to kiss him until her lips were weak, but managed to control herself. 'But, I — I don't und — '

'You don't understand, I know,' he finished for her. 'It is simple. When we marry I want money for you.' He shrugged. 'I work, but money not enough for my English wife. I shall sell and get more. You see.'

So that was it. Money for their wedding. Her eyes widened in their blueness in mock anger. 'No, I do not see, Mr. Tomas Da Silva. I will not let you sell it. You don't have to sell your boat to marry me. I know what it means to you.' Her eyes softened. 'You're wonderful for thinking of me like that, but I can't allow you to do that on my account. I'll marry you and the boat.'

For a moment she did not know whether he was offended or not, an expression of fierce pride clouding his face temporarily. Then it was gone, leaving him serious but a passionate gleam appearing in the brown gaze. 'In Portugal,' he said huskily, 'we have a tradition of punishing ladies who tell the man what he should do.'

'Oh.' Her utterance was a croak of love and desire as his fingertips caressed her cheek to linger on the side of her throat.

'Yes, we love them until they cry for mercy. That is their punishment.'

Pippa's lower body had turned to a jelly. She hoped that sort of punishment would begin and continue all their married life. If only that particular day would go on and on. 'Then,' she said echoing his manner, 'I shall have to risk incurring that punishment.' She made an effort to struggle away from his eyes, grasped the pen and scribbled wildly across the square of cardboard.

Tomas let go one of her hands and stood up, still holding on to her other. 'Then we go back to the boat which is not for sale.' He looked down on her with a wide smile and began to lead her out. Pippa followed, aware of the relief with which Tomas threw the cardboard into the waste bin.

9

Outside, the shadows were lengthening as they walked hand in hand in an excited contentment across the emptying terrace and stood together looking out over the beach. How many times, Pippa thought, had she stood there thinking of Tomas, looking for him by his fishing boat? Now as if by a miracle he was at her side, the man she was going to marry.

She gazed at the yacht which had brought them, like a blue bird sitting easily upon the slight swell of the sea. It would always have a special place in her heart, being the craft in which Tomas had proposed to her.

Suddenly Tomas smacked his free hand against his thigh. 'You know something, Pippa?' She saw the good-humoured puckering of his forehead. 'I forgot the car in Allemura.'

'So had I, Tomas,' she admitted. Quite forgotten about it. Saw his slow smile forming. In love she returned his smile, their eyes locked.

'There is a great excuse for me forgetting, my Pippa,' he said. 'When a man asks a woman to marry him he forgets such things.'

'So does the woman,' laughed Pippa lightly. 'We're both to blame. What shall we do?'

Tomas thought a moment. 'We can walk to Allemura on the path by the cliffs,' he said decisively. 'You like that, maybe quicker.'

Pippa nodded enthusiastically, pleased that he had decided to walk over to Allemura. She felt that she could not trust herself on the boat alone with him again. Neither, she thought, could she trust her stomach after that last drink, not wanting to be seasick and make a fool of herself.

It was her turn to remember something. 'My shopping, Tomas — it's on the boat. I've got my handbag but

I've left the presents.'

Tomas looked away at his boat, smiled reassuringly. 'All right, I fetch them tomorrow. They're safe. I locked the cabin.'

'Will the boat be all right there, Tomas?'

He chuckled at her anxiety. 'This water as good as that,' nodding into the distance towards where the boat had been moored near Allemura when they first boarded it earlier in the afternoon.

Pippa watched as he regarded the stretch of sea seriously. 'No bad weather coming yet, Pippa. Not like England, huh?'

'No,' she agreed, looking in wonderment at the blue late afternoon sky and the contented earth beneath it. Suddenly just for a fleeting moment she was saddened. The thought of the presents had done it. How strange it felt to be talking of presents if she were not going back home. She determined that she must make her mind up about that very soon, but for now she would forget it and enjoy the hours with the man by her side.

They left the terrace and set off across the beach to the beginning of the cliffs. That walk round to Allemura was full of halts for loving kisses under a cooling sun, and of passionate embraces in private corners. And Tomas lifting her over sharp impeding rocks and steadying her on the uneven path.

As she followed him down one very narrow path hand in hand, she wondered when he actually intended to marry her. A week, a month, when? He had not mentioned any particular date yet. She would like to know soon. She would need new clothes and to do all the things that a woman had to do before her wedding. She was not sure about anything really.

The whole thing seemed just an unreal, romantic dream. Could still not quite believe what had happened to her.

They came to where the path broadened and Tomas turned and caught her to him again. After a few moments she eased her mouth reluctantly away from his, asked breathlessly, 'When shall we get married, Tomas my love?' Something unreadable flickered across his face behind the passsion. Doubt, unease? It surprised her. She searched his face, a tremor of anxiety running through her. 'A woman likes to know,' she said, trying to persuade herself that she had mistaken his expression of a few minutes before.

'I make arrangements — tell you soon,' he shrugged, gave a smile — a strangely quick one for him. 'Things to do,' he muttered as he buried his face in her neck.

But Pippa had caught the note of uncertainty and had to reassure herself. Moved her head away. 'You see, Tomas, I have to make arrangements. What about my dress — my wedding dress? What about that? What shall I wear?'

Tomas stepped back, held her at arms' length and to her joyful relief there was no mistaking his expression

185

this time. 'The dress of my country, Pippa, meu bem. You will be the most beautiful bride in all Portugal. You will look magnificent. The dress against your hair and eyes . . . no man will be prouder or love his bride more than I that day.'

'Oh, Tomas,' she gasped, 'I love you. What will the dress be like?'

'Preto — er black with . . . '

'Black!' exclaimed Pippa in great surprise. Black was for funerals.

'You not like black?' He regarded her with some concern.

'It's just that I — well, I never thought of black for a wedding dress.' She laughed quietly. 'I've never been married before, Tomas, in white or black.'

Humour glinted in his gaze. 'Then for the first and last time in your life, meu bem, better that you wear black — it is Portuguese dress.' He shrugged. 'Some women now marry in white, it is modern but . . . ' He grimaced, showing Pippa exactly what he thought of that new idea. He was obviously conservatively minded when it came to wedding attire for a bride.

They kissed again, long and lingering, then started off once more, the path narrowing so much that they walked in single file, he leading, hand tight around hers.

Pippa's doubts about Tomas of a few minutes ago had vanished. The uncertainty he had shown was only about the actual date of the marriage and not that he was having second thoughts on the matter.

She spoke at his back as they descended. 'Which church shall we be married at, Tomas?'

He looked over his shoulder smiling. 'Igreja da goncola.'

'In English please, my love,' she said with a mock severity of tone and a squeeze of his hand.

He continued to look back at her. 'The church — ' Suddenly his hand was jerked from hers as he staggered then fell, to land heavily some yards away against a rock at the side of the path.

Pippa gave a startled cry and scrambled down after him, calling his name over and over. She reached him, knelt beside him, patted his face, her own intensely fearful as she gazed down upon him.

Suddenly, startling her, his eyes were open, deep brown and fully alert. 'Ah, you do love me, Pippa. I hear it in your voice, see it in your face.'

'You're not hurt?' Surprise and great relief stood out on her face, mixed with some irritation that he should have teased her like that.

He moved his head sideways against the rock. 'I look at you instead of my feet — my fault, punished for looking at a beautiful woman.'

She continued to gaze upon him, saw his eyes take in the downward swell of her dress. Shook her head and sighed deeply. 'I thought you were injured or worse.'

A mischievous light grew alongside

the desire in his regard of her. 'You ask me which church — remember?'

She nodded, love bared in her expression. 'I tell you Pippa, now. I cannot fall any further. Igreja da sao goncola — in Allemura.'

'Oh.' She was no wiser.

'Yes, he is the saint who watches over lovers and marriages.'

Tomas's arms suddenly came up and crushed her to him, sprawling her upon him, his mouth working on hers. Then in one forceful movement he turned her and brought her beneath him, his hard masculine body holding her down helplessly.

The uneven ground was hurting her back, but passion was mounting in her body, too. The wedding, the wedding, the thought clamoured in her head. They must wait. His hands were beginning to search . . .

'People,' she gasped, 'someone coming.' She felt his weight easing from her as he raised himself. 'I heard voices.' She hadn't but it had stopped him. Half rolling away from him, she scrambled to her feet and he followed, looking about him.

Seeing no one he eyed her wryly, a humorous light beginning to supplant the dull one of desire. 'You very clever woman, Pippa. First you make me fall in love with you, then you make me think people are coming when they are not.' Shook his head wonderingly. 'Truly I have been caught in a she devil's net.'

'You are the fisherman — not me,' she retorted laughing. Their gaze met and locked and she was alone in the world with him again. Forced herself to look away after a few moments to glance at the path ahead of them. 'Hadn't we better carry on?'

Tomas breathed deeply, the gladitorial slabs of chest muscle outlined against his shirt. 'I think so, Pippa meu bem,' and he sighed reluctantly.

Pippa turned to lead the way, but Tomas grasped her hand. 'I will show you.'

They continued on their way, the path becoming more gradually inclined towards a platform of rocks below. In the near distance she could see the beginning of the long stretch of beach leading to Allemura.

Her eyes fastened on Tomas's strong shoulders, his shirt narrowing loosely downwards to his waist. She had felt the tremendous mounting desire in him firing her own a few minutes before. Twice in the last few hours she had come very close to giving herself to him. She could never live without him now, but her love affair had been a wild scatterbrained thing so far. Did a doubt as to the wisdom of it still exist in her mind? She did not wish to dwell upon it and yet . . . 'Tomas, don't look round. You might fall again, but I'm going to ask another question.' Heard his chuckle.

'All right, I look in front and listen to you.'

'Well, if I do not go home first, where shall I live until we are married?' She

191

could not quite keep the note of anxiety out of her voice.

They had almost reached the platform of rocks and Tomas waited until they were on it before he replied. Then drawing her alongside him he put his arm around her waist as they continued their walk. 'You will live in my house with me.' His tone and glance implied his surprise that she should have had to ask the question.

'Your house?' Her face mirrored her sudden doubt.

'Oh, you have not to worry,' he said with some amusement. 'I have two rooms.' The glint in his dark eyes became brighter. 'You have resisted me so far. I think you will until we marry.' He butterfly kissed her hair, as she felt the colour flooding her face.

They continued onwards, Pippa leaning against him and very busy indeed with her thoughts. It should have come as no surprise to her that he would want her to live under his roof. When her money was exhausted, she would not be able to afford to stay anywhere else.

Strange how a person's attitudes changed. A week ago she would have done anything to gain his attention. Now when he had asked her to marry him — she was behaving prudishly. Girls she knew at work lived openly with their men friends with no thoughts of marriage at all. But Pippa knew herself as a romantic, perhaps old-fashioned, colouring the dowdy things of life whenever possible. She wanted to live the dream of girlhood, to meet the prince of love, be courted, swept up and married to live in the castle of happiness for ever. She had her prince, the promise of marriage, and maybe the date of the latter not far away. She would have to make the best of things until then.

They descended from the flat rocks on to the sand, the wide beach curving slightly into the distance where the fishing boats lay drawn up on the shore. Tomas began to run along the edge of the water pulling her with him and getting ever faster until she could hardly keep up with him, laughing and calling on him to stop. He looked backwards seeing her dress moulding against her thighs, her breasts bobbing in movement. They came to a breathless halt and he let her go, she sinking to the sand, her body heaving. 'I haven't run like that for a long time,' she gasped. She felt alive, reborn in the sound of the waves.

Tomas came and stood astride her looking down on her. Like a straight pine tree towering above, blotting out the sun. That was what he was, she thought — her sun. Her world revolved around him now. She was faintly surprised when he extended his hand to help her to her feet, but then she saw why — some people were approaching.

They started along the beach again, occasionally passing the lonely figure of a man sat on a bucket looking like a rock sculpture, still, and holding his rod, the line disappearing dozens of yards away in the water. Pippa thought these shore fishermen were like dark street bollards placed at intervals. How on earth they caught anything sitting so far back from the water was a puzzle to her.

They reached fisherman's beach and Pippa saw that the fish market had closed. But men still leaned over the sea wall and talked, and a few holiday-makers stood about by the boats in the evening sun. As she and Tomas threaded their way between them she turned to him. 'On the way back will you show me where I — er, we shall live, Tomas? Are you able to see it from the road?' she observed his momentary frown and hesitation and wondered.

He nodded quickly, not looking at her, and striding out in front of her still holding her hand. He muttered something she did not understand. For some reason or other, he appeared reluctant to show her his home. He had told her it had two rooms, but that was all she knew about it, apart from it being somewhere near Allemura. Was he ashamed of it? Didn't he know that she loved him enough to live anywhere with him?

On the way back Pippa could not rid herself of the idea that when they reached her hotel she would say goodbye to Tomas and that would be that. Just a holiday romance over and done with. She would begin her packing that evening ready for the departure the next day. She glanced at the dark ruggedly handsome Portuguese at her side to remind herself that she was indeed going to marry him. He seemed withdrawn, driving automatically, busy in his mind.

In a very short time they were at the crossroads and turning left up the hill to her hotel, a small cloud of dust rising behind them from the road. Tomas brought the car to rest under the covered entrance in front of the huge glass doors, a dirty small car — mouse-like before the impressive hotel.

Pippa suddenly realised that he had

not pointed out where he lived. He may have forgotten, but she guessed that he had refrained from doing so deliberately. Never mind, it would be her home before very long.

She turned to him as he pulled on the hand brake. 'Thank you, dearest Tomas, for such a happy day. I do love you. I shall remember this day all my life.' Saw his eyes glow darkly in the dim light of the car interior.

'The day is not over yet, meu bem,' he said softly. 'You come down to the beach later. I go out with the boat again.' A small smile came and went, 'this time to work.'

She had forgotten. He still had to work, go out that night. Their day together was not over yet. It must last as long as possible. It was a magical day. 'Of course I'll come — I'd forgotten. I was being selfish in not realising that you are not on holiday.'

His expression became serious, grave almost as he gazed for some moments at her. 'You will come, meu bem. You will not leave tonight and fly home to England?'

She stared back at him, all her love for him reflected by the lights in the hotel foyer. 'No, of course not,' she whispered as to a child, deeply comforting. 'You are my home now, Tomas. This will be my home here in Portugal with you.'

They kissed passionately but then a taxi drew up behind them illuminating the inside of the car. Pippa got out then leaned in again for a touching of lips. 'See you at eight, my love.'

'Sao goncola look after you, meu bem,' he replied huskily.

She watched him drive away, suddenly fearful for him as he turned a corner one hand on the wheel, the other still saluting her. The noisy scruffy car was an opulent shiny limousine bearing her Prince away.

10

Inside the hotel again Pippa made straight for her room, hardly conscious of the other people in the lift on the way up. Turning the key in her door she stepped inside, closed it behind her. How long it seemed since she had left the room that morning. All sorts of things had happened to her. An unbelievable, eventful day.

She decided to have a shower, slipping off her dress, seeing the creases. Real passion had formed beneath it that day. Afterwards she lay on the bed in a dreamy state of tired contentment. It was still warm, and the muted sounds of the hotel and its environs floated up through the open balcony door.

Pippa glanced at the watch — six-thirty. Half an hour's rest and then she would dress and go down to see Tomas off. Her thoughts drifted lazily on, enjoyable in their sensations of the new love.

Some while later she opened her eyes. Remembered. It was ten to eight! Throwing her clothes on, she blessed the fact that it was night — he would not see her untidyness, nor the residue of sleep in her eyes. In fact he would see nothing of her if she did not get a move on.

She hurried through the foyer. Perhaps there would be a taxi waiting outside. To her annoyance there was not. Only empty parked cars to one side of the entrance. She could ask reception to telephone for one, but by the time it came she could be down at the beach. A stray dog squatting on the green in front of the hotel looked at her as she went by. Poor little thing, she thought, it had no need to rush — nobody wanted it.

She arrived hot and breathless at the beach to find Tomas and the boats gone, bobbing lights out on the water showing where they were. Running down to the water's edge Pippa tried to penetrate the darkness, catch a glimpse of Tomas — let him know she had come, and had kept her word.

A few of the boats were not too far out yet, perhaps a hundred and fifty yards away — it was difficult to judge accurately. She stood and waved, a light coloured figure alone at the sea's edge. Then on one of the shadowy shapes somewhat to her right a light began to swing to and fro as if held by a hand. Her heart gave a jump. Was that Tomas answering her? She glanced at the other lights. They were going up and down gently, not one was moving sideways. It must be Tomas. Relief that he knew she was there filled her, and she continued to wave until the light stopped its sideways motion and became just one of the many steadily shining dots above the sea.

Afterwards she dined in the restaurant at the rear of the terrace café where she and Tomas had sat that afternoon.

Then she made her way slowly back to the hotel and her room. There she sat on the balcony looking out at the still visible lights of the fishing fleet. One of those was the lamp of love hovering over the man she was to marry.

It was too early to go to bed and in any case Pippa knew she would not sleep. He mind was too full — so many thoughts. Tomas was hers. She smiled proudly to herself. All the holiday makers in the hotel would go home sometime. Perhaps remember their stay there or forget in the years to come. Whereas she, with her love for Tomas and their forthcoming marriage had formed a bond with the country. She would become part of its life, its customs.

Her mind went back to the day a month before when she had slipped into the travel agent's office during her lunch time. The agent had flicked through his pages doubtfully. 'A single room — hmmm, bit difficult to get at short notice.' A few more pages turned then his hand had rested. 'There's the Monte Sirocco, might manage one there.' He looked up at her, turning the brochure the other way round between them on the counter, his finger pointing at a picture of a hotel at the top of the page.

Pippa had studied it. A large white balconied building with the usual swimming pool in front of it. She saw the heading above it. The Algarve. 'The Algarve?' she had queried, not quite sure where it was.

'Southern Portugal, it's very nice, and that hotel's good, though maybe a bit pricier than some. I can ring through — get confirmation. That all right for you?'

She had decided there and then that it would be, and so to the Algarve she had been transported. Pippa smiled wonderingly at the stars. An agent's finger resting on one hotel amongst hundreds. Of such chance things were romantic encounters born.

Her thoughts turned to that day with

him — that special day nearly ended. Saw again the guarded look that had come and gone swiftly in the café when she had casually mentioned that he seemed to know a lot about wine. Simple fisherman he might be on the surface, but a good deal more sophisticated than she had at first supposed. Many things about him still puzzled her.

The faint drone of a distant plane disturbed her thoughts and reminded her of the decision to be made before she met him again in the morning. Whether she should go home or not. Subconsciously she had wrestled with the problem ever since his proposal of marriage. Now she realised there was only one thing she could do, she must go home first. Fly home as planned tomorrow night, then return at the earliest opportunity to marry him. She just could not possibly stay in Portugal and get married without explaining to her mother and putting things in order at home. Even if it were only for a week. There was also the fact that there may be some money to come to her from work, and every little would help when she and Tomas married.

Pippa sighed deeply in the turmoil of her thoughts. Her mind would be much easier when she knew that she would be leaving her mother well cared for. And anyway, she consoled herself, their parting would not be forever. As Tomas had said, her mother could come to Portugal. After all she wasn't that old. The marriage would come as a shock to her, but she would get over it. Pippa's eyes misted over obscuring the lights of the fishing fleet. In the morning she would tell Tomas of her decision.

She left the balcony and went into the bedroom. Now that love had come to her, did it have to be so worrysome? So full of joy one moment, sadness and misgivings the next?

After breakfast the next morning she went straight back to her room to pack her bag. It had to be vacated before noon. She dressed for the day, knowing that she would have no time or chance to change clothes later. White slacks, a green, quarter-sleeved open necked top and a white lightweight jacket completed her ensemble. Inside her small travelling bag was a cream plastic raincoat and also a pair of stout shoes for when she arrived back in Manchester to replace the sandals that she now wore.

She rang for the porter to take her cases downstairs, then took a last glance back into the room. Fears, hope, joy, had all shared it with her during that holiday. In the foyer she handed in her keys, the number was imprinted on her memory. Settled her account, then watched as her luggage was put away ready to be transferred to the coach later that afternoon. Someday she and Tomas would come there to that hotel and she would remember everything. Would see the envious stares of the women as she walked proudly at his side.

She set off down the road from the

hotel, hearing the voices and splashes coming already from the swimming pool. The air was warm with a gentle breeze, and the climbing sun shone directly on her. Joy was in her heart but also some apprehension at the thought of telling Tomas that she had decided to go home before marrying him. But could he really have expected her to turn her back immediately and perhaps finally on her family without seeing them again?

Tomas was waiting for her, leaning against the side of his boat with, from a distance at least, the air of a man who has unlimited time to do what he wanted. He caught sight of her, waved, becoming upright, his gaze intent upon her.

She reached the wooden kiosk, went down the steps and on to the sand. Her heart began to leap in anticipation of meeting him again. What would he say when he heard that she was going home?

He stood poised with the eager

expectancy of a lover. Pippa could not see his expression fully under the tilted peak of his cap, but guessed that he was observing her every movement. A streak of sensual pleasure ran from her thighs to the pit of her stomach, making her tremble slightly as she approached him. Momentarily she stopped in front of him. Saw the controlled passion in his dark face, the look of a man seeing his love for the first time in a few long hours.

She felt almost shy after the extravagant words and emotions of the day before. It was almost like a replay of their earlier meeting when she had prayed that he would return her feelings. Almost, with the difference now that a miracle had happened and they were to be married.

'Pippa, meu bem.' His voice was husky and soft against the murmuring of the sea. A deep excitement ran through it, echoing that coursing through her body at his greeting.

'Tomas, meu bem,' she returned

tremulously, her breathing suddenly very shallow. She saw him glance up towards the terrace which was becoming busy as mid morning approached. Then without saying anything else and to her surprise he took her by the arm and ushered her towards the steps she had just descended. Together they climbed to the comparative privacy of the veranda in front of the shuttered kiosk. Pippa remembered how they had sat there in conversation the day before. Was it only yesterday? And Tomas had taken her for the sail afterwards.

She folded into his arms. 'I did come last night, Tomas. I dozed off on the bed. Then I rushed down but you'd gone,' she explained breathlessly under his tightening embrace. 'Did you see me? I waved to you at the water's edge.'

'You were in white — like now.'

She nodded. 'Yes, and you waved a lamp. You did see me then?'

'Sim — yes.' His mouth was close to hers, impatient for its prey. And the pressure of his hands on her back curved her body brutally to his. The sunny day dimmed as she closed her eyes. Her knees would have buckled if she had not wound her arms around his neck. They drifted in the wonderland of their kiss, for how long Pippa did not know or care, but then the steps vibrated and noisy voices drew near quickly.

Her eyes fluttered open and she withdrew her lips reluctantly. Two young boys, all arms and legs and rush, gained the top of the steps and vanished round the corner of the kiosk without giving the lovers a chance. A suck of the iced lolly was sweeter to them than the most passionate kiss of their elders.

The interruption prompted Pippa to remember what she must tell Tomas. She drew back to look at him, feeling his hands slowly withdrawing from around her until they rested upon her hips. Some nervousness began to replace her erstwhile ecstacy. 'Tomas, she ventured, 'I've something to tell you. I — I've decided. I'm going home first. I have to.'

Alertness returned to his eyes swiftly, their expression the nearest to anger she had ever seen. Then it was gone suddenly, leaving one of stern disapproval as he continued to stare silently at her for long moments.

'I'll be back,' she said earnestly, guessing his thoughts. 'Perhaps a week — not much longer.'

His hands left her. 'You say perhaps.' He shrugged. 'Perhaps never. England will hold you — you will forget.'

'No, that's not true, Tomas,' Pippa retorted vehemently. 'I love you more than anything. Haven't I promised to marry you? But don't you realise I cannot just disappear from home. My mother is not well.'

Her companion seemed somewhat surprised at the strength of her reply. 'Ah, your mother,' he nodded understandingly. 'I forget.'

Pippa wished she had not mentioned her. Somehow it had taken a little of the magic from the morning. She was also saddened and irritated at the fact that her mother should have come into the argument.

They stood apart regarding each other, an impasse of a sort between them. Pippa was the first to speak in a gentle, reassuring tone. 'Look, Tomas, my love, I shall be leaving the hotel at about four-thirty. Why don't you take me now to where we shall live when we are married? I'd love to see it. Then I can picture it when I am home.'

Once more she saw the unreadable shadow flit across his dark features. He gave a twisted smile, said lightly, 'Perhaps bad luck for the bride to see home before marriage, eh?'

Behind his attempted lightness Pippa sensed an uneasiness. 'I'm sure that can't be true,' she protested, smiling. 'Most brides in England see their house before they are married. It's part of the fun, I think.' She paused, then asked, 'Don't you want me to see it?' Her blue eyes were compelling in their directness and frankness. Before he could answer a sudden awful thought gripped her. 'You're not married already, Tomas?' Her fear went as quickly as it had come as he laughed shortly but with genuine humour. It was good to see the gleam in his eyes again.

'You not think much of Portuguese men if you believe that,' he smiled wryly.

Suddenly the awkwardness was gone from between them, the tenseness vanishing. 'I love one of them anyway,' she whispered.

They would have fallen into each other's arms again but a party of several people rounded the kiosk corner. Pippa saw his fleeting annoyance, said, 'Never mind, when we are married there will be no interruptions.' Took his hand in hers. 'Now, Tomas, m-meu bem,' saw the smile at her pronunciation, 'if you will not show the house, at least tell me about it. Is it a terrace, a little house, a semi?' Did they have semis in Portugal? Her eyes danced mischievously, 'or are you going to put me in a tent on the beach?'

The look that he gave her made her think that she would submit there and then to his love-making, but he surprised her by answering in a similar fashion though the light of desire lingered in his eyes. 'I think the only place to keep you is a castle — well guarded from other men.' Then he grimaced, shook his head. 'No, not a castle — too uncomfortable, a palace perhaps.' His face assumed a mock sternness, 'But still well guarded.'

'And what about you, where would you be?' Pippa asked smiling.

'I should visit you every day and every night.' He reached out and with the back of his hand pushed her hair back from the side of her face, then with fingers and palm lightly stroked her cheek and down to the base of her throat. His look had become serious, intense under some strong emotion. He went on quietly. 'I look in papers, I see princess here — princess there in photographs. They have no right to be called princess — they are ugly, vain, money instead of a heart.' He tapped her cheek lightly. 'But you — you deserve to be one. You are a real princess to me.'

Pippa leaned against him, she couldn't help it. Looked up at him with love's eyes. 'You know, Tomas, apart from you asking me to marry you, that's the nicest thing you've ever said to me.' She moved her head on him. 'The nicest thing that anybody has ever said to me.'

His lips pressed into her hair, then she heard him sigh deeply and gently. He put his arm through hers and began to lead her round the corner of the kiosk. His voice was thick and unsteady. 'I think I take you to look at the house. It will be our house. If I do not you will torment me for the rest of the day. Being a woman you are curious and I must at least get rid of your curiosity.' He put his arm around her. 'Would that make my princess happy?'

Her love shone brightly blue as she answered softly, 'You don't have to, my love, but if you did my happiness will be complete, though I don't think I could be happier than I am now.' And that was the truth she knew. His arm tightened until she thought her ribs would crack. They came abreast of the terrace, he then contenting himself with holding her hand.

Suddenly he touched his forehead with his fingers. 'I forget. Wait,' he told her and disappeared back down to the beach again. She saw him go up to his boat, reach in and bring out a bag. He reappeared a few seconds later and handed it to her. It was her shopping from the day before. Her presents. She'd forgotten about them. He had retrieved them from his sailing boat as he had promised he would. 'I hope that you do not need them, but . . . ' He shrugged regretfully.

'It won't be for long, Tomas,' she said comfortingly. 'I shall not stay away any longer than I need to.' She was glad that he had not been too obstructive about her returning home. 'Now take me to this house. I'm so excited. I can't wait to see it.'

She tucked her arm through his as they went towards his car, the hardness of his thigh moving against hers giving her a sensual pleasure. 'Tomas,' she said without looking at him, 'your English is getting better and better each day I've noticed.'

His voice was casual and she felt the slight raising of his shoulders. 'I talk to you an English lady, so my English improves.' She glanced at him as they got into the car. His reply had been easy — too easy. She was not convinced by it and wondered again.

11

After a few minutes she realised they were heading in the direction of Allemura. Reaching it, Tomas turned the car right and away from the busy main street, Pippa glimpsing the pale faces of the newly arrived holiday makers.

The street that they took was narrower being little more than a bus width, and climbed gently with shops and bars with dark interiors on either side.

Another hundred yards and the shops became fewer, and Pippa guessed this was the older part of the town. Mostly terraced houses lined the road in a parade of coloured tiles, each house front covered in them in a pleasing and individual way. A striking contrast to the monotonous blue of the sky. Ahead, Pippa caught sight of a white church tower and its clock showing two forty-five. She must not be too long.

Small streets shot off at all angles now and Tomas stopped the car at the entrance to one of them. He got out and she followed, glancing about her with an excited expectancy. He waited until she was alongside of him then he nodded at a building ahead of them.

Pippa saw a small house flat roofed and square, the end one of a short row, blue tiled in the mid blue she had seen so often as paintwork. A light brown door with a window either side — each one heavily shuttered in the same colour. Above, a small balcony — white railed. Beyond it in the shade another window shuttered like the ones below. To the right of the balcony a short flight of steps led to the roof.

She continued to gaze at it — one up, one down. A living room and a bedroom above.

'You disappointed?' Tomas's tone indicating that he had expected her to be.

She glanced at him quickly to find him eyeing her keenly. 'No, no, Tomas, it's very nice — just that I didn't know what to expect. Everything is strange to me.' Pippa sensed that he was already regretting bringing her there. She went up to the house, let her fingers slide gently down the shutters as if awakening a sleeping eye. Grasped the sloping door handle lightly.

'It is not ready for a woman yet. I have it ready for when you come back.'

She smiled round at him in resigned agreement. It was plain that he did not want her to go inside. She was disappointed. But what had she expected?

He was a fisherman, and fishermen did not own large modern and expensive villas. She loved him though, and that was all that mattered. If she put her mind to it she would be happy there and make Tomas a good wife, and bring life and love to the house. If she married him she must live where he did, and that was that.

Turning to him she said cheerfully, all trace of her disapointment gone, 'I shall enjoy it here with you, Tomas, I know I shall.' As she spoke she glimpsed behind him a woman's face and the flutter of a curtain through a half open shutter. How would she get on with the people round about? Would the women accept her?

'What is the matter?' asked Tomas, noticing a change in her expression.

'Oh, nothing, Tomas. I saw someone, a woman watching us. I just hope I can get on with them when I live here.'

He shrugged, smiled. 'A woman is curious. It will give them something to talk about.' His expression became stern, 'But it is up to them to get on with you, meu bem.' Relaxing in manner again he went on, 'I see only little of them. I sleep here then I fish. They do not see me much.' He put an arm around Pippa's shoulders. 'I make sure that they are good to you,' he said in a menacing voice, but she saw the upwards curve of his lips.

They strolled towards the car again and Pippa glanced back at the house. It was a pretty little one really, and the main road was visible from it. She would not feel as cut off as she would have been living in an enclosed square. She noticed the name of the street on the wall. Rua de novembo Vinte e Dois. She guessed the twenty-second of November street. As they reached the car she caught sight of the church tower again. 'Are we going to be married in that church?'

He hesitated slightly. 'Yes, I think so.'

'Well, it's certainly near enough to our house isn't it?' How strange it seemed to be talking of their house, she thought. 'Can I just look at the outside please, Tomas?'

He looked deeply into her face for a few moments and she was surprised at the dancing humour in his eyes. 'Yes, Miss Pippa and then I shall take you to Faro, Loule, Portimao, Albufeira, Montechoro, Silves, Sagres. I shall be

Tomas the courier.'

Pippa laughed at his joking, slapped his arm playfully. 'Just the church will do, Tomas.'

His arm left her shoulders, grasped her hand as they began to walk towards the church some hundred yards further up to where the road began to curve. 'Always it is busy when I want to kiss you,' he lamented.

'Perhaps it is just as well,' she replied. She had felt the strength of the pressure of his hand over hers. Suddenly it struck her that he must be tired having been fishing for most of the night — he would not have slept yet that day. 'Tomas, you poor thing, no wonder you did not want to be dragged about. You haven't been to bed yet — you must be tired.'

He shrugged and smiled rather sadly. 'Later, when you are gone.'

Yes, when she was gone. It was like a dream she thought, to end abruptly when she came into England in a few hours' time. But it was not a dream.

223

The man by her side was proof of that, and just further up the road was the church where she would probably be married.

The church stood in a square facing on to the street, a squat, white unpretentious building with a sun dried, dark double door. Its tower rose four sided to a pyramid top. Pippa saw the bell hanging, silhouetted, and still in the open belfry and the straight flight of unsheltered steps leading to it. Would that bell ring for her on her wedding day? The clock that she had seen earlier now reminded her that she must return to the hotel.

Nearing the car again Pippa asked, 'What is the church called, Tomas?'

'Sao Sebastiao.' He saw her brow wrinkle. 'Saint Sebastian, I think you say in England.'

'Ah, yes.' She must try and remember all these things.

They set off threading their way back down the narrow streets to join the main road which would take them to Monte Sirocco. A silence fell between them and Pippa observed that Tomas wore a troubled, withdrawn expression. She herself was beginning to feel despondent. Soon they were to part.

Tomas stopped the car in sight of the hotel and opposite some spare land, then turned to her. 'Now I say goodbye here, Pippa, meu bem.' He took her in his arms and hers went tightly round his neck, her eyes moist. 'I love you, Tomas with all my heart, I'll be back soon. I'll never stop thinking of you whilst I'm away. You've made my life wonderful.'

'You forgive me for what I did?'

She realised he was referring to keeping her in the apartment. 'A thousand times.' A bus passed drowning his next words. Then his lips sealed hers, travelled down her throat until they touched the tips of her breasts through her dress. She did not resist but clutched his dark head to her. 'Thank you for taking me to the house and church today. I shall be able to tell my mother all about it; she will want to know everything.'

Tomas lifted his head slowly, his eyes glowing darkly. 'You will tell her that I am a good man, eh? Will look after you.'

'You're more than that, my love — you're my world.'

'I will arrange day of wedding when you are away, Pippa, meu bem.

He put a hand into his jacket, brought out a piece of paper, gave it to her. 'Telephone from airport when you come back. I fetch you.'

'I'll write as soon as I know when I'm returning.'

They kissed again. 'Oh, Tomas, I don't want to leave you but I must,' she said sighing and drawing away. Tomas turned the ignition key with an unsteady hand.

Before she had hardly time to straighten her dress they had reached the hotel. She leaned across for a last kiss. 'Wait a minute then turn and I'll watch you go from my balcony.' A sudden fear for him overcame her. 'You will be careful on the sea, my love — promise me,' she beseeched him.

He nodded, a trace of a smile appearing. 'I have two friends — one is the sea, I respect it. The other is you and I love you.' He went on in a voice which caressed her ears. 'One thing, meu bem, I wish to do in my life and that is to marry you, so I take no risk.' As she got out he called after her, 'You come back to me, meu bem.'

She drew a shuddering breath, looked back in. 'I will, I will, Tomas.'

She was halfway along the corridor towards room Three-Two-Six when she realised with a slight shock that it was not hers any longer. She had vacated the room according to the hotel rules by midday, and had handed her keys in at the reception desk. What about the roof garden?

Hurrying back to the lift, she ascended to the top floor. Thankfully there was no one about, and she dashed to the parapet overlooking the road. How small everything looked. She searched the road. A car was going away from the hotel slowly. Thought it was Tomas's car. Waved. Would he look back and up to the roof?

The car she was observing stopped, and a figure appeared through its roof. She saw a movement of an arm. Tomas standing on the seat, his body through the sun roof. 'Tomas,' she shouted against the strong breeze and waving both arms vigorously. Four stars and a plus hotel or not she was saying goodbye as promised, even though it was not from where she had expected to do it.

She was glad he had seen her. Then his figure disappeared and the car moved off getting smaller until it reached the crossroads and waited to turn right. She saw the brake lights go out and the tiny dot lost to sight behind some buildings.

Her tears fell over the parapet as she leaned on it. They would think it was raining down below! Afterwards she went into the women's room, washed her face, then went into the foyer to wait with the others for the airport coach.

12

Pippa stared out from her window seat into the purple night above the clouds. Try as she might to reject it, jealousy was striking through her mind. Had Tomas turned the corner and gone straight home to be with Carmella? No doubt the latter would find out that she — Pippa — had gone home, and would renew her attempts to turn Tomas's attentions upon herself. Pippa had given no thought to Carmella during the last few days but now when she was alone on the plane, the face of Carmella was beginning to haunt her.

Doubt and fears crowded in. She remembered his reluctance to show her the house. When she had persisted in the matter he had taken her, but had not shown her the interior. It was going to be her home and would not a prospective bridegroom expect his bride to wish to see inside her future home? Or was it really that he had no intention of marrying her after all? But had he not said that he would arrange for the wedding whilst she was in England? How could he though when he did not know the date of her return to Portugal? Could it be that he had lost interest in her when she did not fall straight into bed with him?

Pippa strove to steady her wild thoughts — to look for and cling to the real facts. He had asked her to marry him. Spoken of his love for her. Wasn't that enough? Also he had asked her to marry him almost immediately and not to go home. That was not the action of a man who was thinking of deceiving her. She was glad when the stewardess brought the trolley round — a drink would help to relieve her gloom and doubts.

For a while afterwards she felt better but then another strange and irrational fear took a hold of her. A fear that she would never return to Portugal. That when she got home the clutching melancholy of the hills would imprison her for the rest of her life. A love hate relationship with her birth place. And the love for Tomas that had flared under the hot sun of Portugal would wither between the dark contours of the Pennines. She would become a spinster looking after an ageing parent — the chance of marriage gone. Real love came perhaps only once — not to find another.

By the time she arrived at Manchester airport, however, she had managed to throw off most of her depression. The bustle, the movement and retrieving of her luggage serving to keep her mind occupied.

Pippa huddled smaller into her coat against the wind and rain as in the darkness she made for the car park. What a change from the light clothing she had worn for the past two weeks fifteen hundred miles away! She was relieved to find that her orange coloured mini was where she had left it, having heard stories of wheels and even engines being stolen whilst the owner was away. Inside, the car was damp and cold and she shivered, the thought coming that she could always sell it to make more money for when she and Tomas married. To have it shipped out there would take an enormous sum and in any case Tomas had a car.

An hour and a half later she entered her home somewhat apprehensively, knowing it was going to be a difficult and painful business explaining everything to her mother. That person welcomed her daughter's return delightedly, Pippa marvelling again at the youthful face of her parent. Only the dark three quarter moons below her eyes and the breathlessness telling of her mother's heart trouble.

She sat down in front of the gas fire holding the first decent cup of tea she'd had since leaving home whilst her mother finished preparing the meal for them. Pippa decided that she would not say anything yet until they had eaten, going over in her mind how to break the news. In one way she was bursting to tell of the marvellous thing that had happened to her, and yet dreading the effect it may have on her mother. But it had to be done. She had to be told.

Mrs. Gentle came out of the kitchen, smiled fondly at her daughter. 'Well, and how was the holiday?'

Pippa looked up at her. 'Marvellous, Mum. It really was fabulous.'

'You certainly look well, you're quite tanned.'

'Oh, Mum, the sun shone every day. Seventy degrees at least and that's their winter,' Pippa informed her enthusiastically.

'And the hotel?'

'Out of this world. You'd have loved it. But I didn't spend much time round the hotel. I went out quite a lot.' Her heart picked up its beat. 'There was a beautiful beach just down the road — I spent a lot of time there. Golden beach it was called — in English anyway. Fishermen's boats and a terrace with a bar and café.' She sighed. 'Then I come back to this weather.'

Her mother smiled knowingly. 'Oh you'll get back into the swing after a few days.' She bent down, kissed Pippa lightly on the cheek. 'It's so nice to have you back, dearest.'

Pippa shrivelled inside herself. Her mother was making it very hard for her.

Over the meal Mrs. Gentle chatted animatedly. She'd had a letter from John. They were all well and might be coming up just before Christmas. The doctor had examined her again and had been satisfied with her general condition, and providing she did not exert herself too much physically and kept clear of worry she should be all right.

Oh dear, thought Pippa. Clear of worry! Her news was not going to help much. She must impress on her mother that she could come and live in Portugal, and that there was no need for them to be separated.

Her mother's voice broke into her thoughts. 'You look far away, Pippa.

Anything the matter?'

'No, no, I — I'm just doing justice to this,' indicating her plate.

Truth to tell, the edge of her appetite had begun to go at the nearing prospect of informing her parent of her plans for the future.

Her mother went on, 'the local forecaster says there's a good chance of snow round about Christmas this year.'

'That's the last thing I want,' said Pippa dismissively. She couldn't begin to think of Christmas, still felt the sun on her face, the kiss on her lips from Tomas as they had parted. She didn't want to think about anything that would draw her back into the life that she knew before she met him. Part of her was still in Portugal — the other struggling not to get too involved again with matters at home. It would make it all the harder when the time came to return to Tomas.

Afterwards they sat by the fire, each with another cup of tea and Pippa putting off the moment when she must tell her mother. She regarded the brown liquid. When she had finished that, then . . .

Mrs. Gentle looked across at her. 'Did you like Portugal, Pippa? Would you go again?'

Now! Now was the opportunity. Her mother had provided it. 'I loved it, Mum.' She hesitated, went on, unable to stop the tremor in her voice. 'I — I shall have to go again.' Saw the slight frown, then the half smile.

'Oh, you mean next year — a long way off. You'll have to save up again.'

Pippa felt the tension mounting. 'No, I — I'm sorry, Mum, but I mean soon. I'm going back soon.'

The face across was still, like a sculptured bust. 'Going back! But — but how d'you mean?' The blue eyes stared incomprehendingly into her own.

Pippa plunged in rushing her words, hoping that by doing so she would lighten the shock. Get it over quickly. 'Oh, Mum, he's lovely. I met him there — Tomas. Asked me to marry him.

He's arranging it, whilst I'm here. He wants you to go over. You'll like him.'

Her mother leaned forward on the edge of her chair, looked away into the fire, her hands tight round her cup. Pippa gazed anxiously at her. All she had dreaded was etched in her mother's face.

After a few moments her mother looked up. 'You met in the hotel, did you?' she asked tonelessly.

'No, we met on the beach.'

'I mean was he on holiday staying in your hotel?'

Pippa heard the slight note of irritation. 'No, he lives in Portugal not far from the hotel.'

'What does he do?'

Pippa took a sip of her tea before answering. 'He's a fisherman,' she stated a trifle defensively, glancing through the window at the rain and greyness. Somehow the sun, warm wind and the coloured boats made fishing a less harsh and more dignified and romantic calling.

'A fisherman!' Her mother's voice had come to life again in something akin to horror.

'It's not like it is here, Mum,' Pippa explained hurriedly. 'He shares a boat for fishing, and he has another one of his own.' Oh, how could she make her mother feel what she herself felt for Tomas? The brown eyes in the stern face searching her mind. Sometimes mocking, sometimes clouded with some trouble. The rare smile, and when it came like a burst of sunshine flooding the room.

She saw the dawning question on her mother's lips. 'Portuguese,' she nodded. 'Yes he is, Mum. Born there, works there and lives there. Yes, he's got to be Portuguese.' Immediately she was sorry for the irritated manner in which she had answered. But you couldn't help things. You fell in love, and that was that.

Mrs. Gentle got up slowly and began to pick up the plates off the table, her back to her daughter.

Pippa stood up and put her arm around her mother's shoulder, felt the slight movement. 'Don't be upset, Mum. The world's a small place now. You can come and live over there. Tomas said he'd like that. It's only two and three-quarter hours away from Manchester airport — it's not long really.'

He mother nodded silently and carried the dishes into the kitchen, and Pippa heard them being put into the sink. She remembered after her father had died, her mother doing the same thing later. Sticking to familiar things, the routine, to mask the heartbreak and occupy her hands if not her mind.

Her mother came out of the kitchen, bent over the table again. 'Tomas,' she murmured as if to herself.

'It's all right, you'll like him. He's not a rough man — he'll look after me.'

'But, Portugal . . . ' A shake of the head.

'It's not far, Mum, not these days. We

240

want you to come. You'll love it. I know you will.'

Worry lines creased her parent's brow. 'There's John and the children to think of.'

Pippa nodded, thinking that perhaps in the future she would in turn have her children to think about. Taking her mother's arm she said, 'Leave the dishes, I'll do them later. Come and sit down again.'

Mrs. Gentle studied her daughter. 'Isn't there someone at work you could fall for?'

Pippa saw the anxiety — an anxiety to keep her at home. It was only natural, she supposed. Might it not have been easier if she'd stayed in Portugal? Done the deed and got married. Just sent a letter or telephoned. She sighed inwardly. The more you thought of other people's feelings the more painful it was for oneself.

Her mother was speaking. 'Strange how it's repeated. My father didn't think your father suitable at all, not at first anyway.' A ghost of a smile appeared and Pippa was glad to see it. 'I knew there was something,' continued Mrs. Gentle reflectively, 'as soon as you came in today. You were worried over something and yet you were excited.'

'You're not angry, Mum?' asked Pippa relieved now at the way things were going. 'I couldn't help it. He was there and that was it, but you'll like him, I promise.'

The older woman looked at the shining eyes, the flushed and radiant face. Her daughter was well and truly in love, and open, vulnerable to hurts. 'Have you a photograph of him?'

The question came as somewhat of a surprise to Pippa. 'No, I haven't.' She smiled ruefully. 'I just never thought about it.' It did seem strange now, but she had forgotten to have the photographs developed that they had taken together on his boat. Perhaps it was because their time together had been so short, their feelings so intense, or that the exchange of photographs would have reminded them too much of the parting to come.

'Oh well,' said her mother with a somewhat forced smile, 'perhaps you can send me one on.'

'Oh I will, don't worry, Mum.' It must be hard for her, thought Pippa to have the news broken so quickly. If only Tomas had come over with her. It would have made things a lot easier. Her mother might have been more satisfied and settled in her mind if he had done so. She hastened to give a mental picture of her beloved and ended by saying, 'and he hasn't got long hair either,' knowing how her mother abhorred long hair on young men.

'Well, he sounds very nice, Pippa. I hope you'll be all right and very happy.' There was a catch in her voice, and Pippa saw the coming loneliness in her eyes.

In an effort to cheer her and herself Pippa said, 'You will come to the wedding, Mum?' Saw the quick doubt in the other. 'You'll be all right. It's just a matter of getting on the plane, and we'll meet you at the other end. I could let you know the date ahead. And don't worry about the money, we'll find some way of helping you.' She didn't know how, but a way would be found. And it would give her mother something to plan for.

Pippa was in bed by eleven, enclosed in a long woollen nightdress and a bottle in the bed, the wall fire fading dully in the darkness. Was it only last night that the balcony window remained open, and the light sheets loose against her naked body? Questions crowded her mind. When would she leave her job? How long would it take to sell her car? Would her mother be able to attend the wedding?

She fell asleep with the tormenting brown eyes of Tomas looking deeply into her own.

13

For Pippa the next day at work had an air of unreality about it. Unable to keep her joyous secret to herself she told one of her friends and soon the rest of the department knew. Questions rained upon her and many were the envious glances. Later in the day she found out that financially it would be better for her to leave at Christmas. She would then be entitled to some holiday payment, on top of what she would earn up to that time. She thought it over as she typed, fingers and brain busy with quite different matters. Three more weeks to Christmas — it seemed such a long time ahead. She had wanted to be done with everything at home and to return to Tomas quickly. It was not quite so simple. The extra money would be very useful and would go some way towards paying for her mother's flight to the wedding, but if she did decide to stay until Christmas she wanted to be away immediately afterwards. That would be it — not one day longer than necessary.

During her lunch break she popped into the travel agent's. Booked the first plane to Faro after Christmas. Twenty to eight in the morning on the Sunday. What an unearthly hour! However, she felt better now that the date of her return had been fixed and would write that night to Tomas and tell him, then he could arrange for the wedding properly. She must remember also to ask him to send a photograph of himself so she could show it to her mother. Pippa shrugged mentally. For herself it did not matter — she had his picture imprinted on her heart.

The weeks to Christmas dragged on. At work try as she might she could not concentrate, making simple mistakes that she would never have done before. The management would think that she did not care any more. It was not that at all, but her mind was full of thoughts about the momentous decision that she had made.

During the second week a letter arrived from Tomas. In it he apologised for not being able to write English as well as he thought he spoke it. He was still making arrangements for their marriage, and would meet her at Faro airport on Sunday the twenty-seventh of December. Pippa read it over and over again. Even allowing for the inability of Tomas to express himself on paper well — the tone of the letter was more formal than she had expected. Disappointments and doubts coursed swiftly through her. He still had not given her the date of their wedding.

Another aspect puzzled her. He had expressed neither surprise nor disappointment at the fact that she was not returning until after Christmas. They had been talking before she left of a matter of a week or so, yet he had accepted her decision without comment. Could his love have cooled so quickly?

The doubts grew very large in the next few days. Was she doing the right thing in returning to Portugal? She loved him achingly, but longing and ardour were it seemed, missing from his letter. She sought consolation in the fact that Tomas was not a demonstrative man, reserved — on the surface anyway. It appeared to be a national characteristic. Alone with him was a very different matter, as she knew. She remembered the one time he had given way to his feelings in public. When she had accepted his proposal on the beach by the boats. How he had picked her up in his arms, and run down to the water in circles with her until she had become dizzy. It all seemed a long time and a long way away now. And yet it had happened.

Mrs. Gentle must have noticed her daughter's pensive and often worried look. 'Is everything all right, dear?' she had said one day. Pippa had expressed a forced cheerfulness in her reply for her mother's sake. She had not shown the latter the letter, but had lied about its contents saying that there was a delay in deciding the date owing to so many weddings previously booked. 'But don't worry, Mum, you're going to be there whatever the date is,' she had assured her. That was, she thought despondently, if there was going to be a wedding at all!

That week Pippa advertised her car for sale in the local paper and sold it for three hundred and seventy-five pounds a day later. She felt that she had done quite well, as the car was several years old.

The same night she wrote again to Tomas telling him of this and also enclosing a photograph of herself. She found it hard to know what to say in her letter, desiring to pour out her heart to him, but the words appearing cold and impersonal when put upon the paper. She tore up several sheets before she finally placed the letter, which read almost as formally as she had adjudged his to be, in the envelope.

Christmas trees began to appear against the walls outside shops and Pippa bought a small one, but it was with some sadness. Partly because probably it would be the last Christmas with her mother and partly because it reminded her of her father. At Christmas he had always bought the tallest tree that would fit into the room, scraping the ceiling. She had loved decorating it.

A few days beforehand it started to snow heavily making the stone walls dividing the fields look like dark Christmas cake with a thick icing. The girls at work presented her with an electric toaster as a wedding present and then they went out to lunch, Pippa getting slightly tipsy as a result. She promised to write to them telling them how she was getting on, and insisting that they visit her if ever they came to that part of Portugal. After the goodbyes she walked home clutching the toaster. First the car, now her work. One by one the ties with her old life were being cut.

Then Tomas's second letter arrived — almost as short and the English just as awkwardly written as in the first. Did he do it on purpose, so that he would have an excuse not to write much? Nevertheless, the tone of the letter was more relaxed, warmer. Pippa read it in the privacy of her bedroom. He was having the photograph that she had taken of him on the boat developed, and would send it on. The house was nearly ready for her. This latter piece of news made her feel a lot better. He ended with his own special term of endearment that he used occasionally for her — 'my little fish' — on account of her being such a good swimmer. There was also something else in Portuguese which she could not understand.

Pippa rested the letter in her lap, stared at it, pleased about the house.

But still there was no mention of a date for their wedding. That meant she would have to return to Portugal unable to give her mother the date. Of course she could always telephone home, but it might be too late for her mother to make arrangements for her to fly out. Did Tomas really want her mother to attend? In fact, did he really intend there to be a wedding at all?

Christmas was a sad, strained time for both Pippa and her mother. The latter putting on a brave face as the day for her daughter's departure drew near.

On the Saturday night preceding her flight, Pippa retired to bed early after seeing that her passport and luggage were ready for the early start on her return journey. She gazed about her room at the things which had been part of her life. School photographs, holiday snapshots. Books, tennis racket, record player, wardrobe of clothes. The old doll's head on the end of her pyjama case lying on her bed as it had done for years. Each and every one evoking some memory. How swiftly things had taken place since she went on holiday a month ago.

In bed she stared over the covers at the circle of green figures on the alarm clock. The taxi was for five o'clock — she must be up for four. Had told her mother to stay in bed.

'I'll get up to see you off, Pippa,' her mother had replied determinedly, her tone brooking no argument.

Pippa awoke at almost four in the morning. Was it a dream she had had? Portugal, Tomas, talk of a wedding . . . Suddenly the alarm shattered the stillness and any doubts vanished in the dark and cold of the room. She crept downstairs, made a cup of tea and took one up to her mother who was awake.

'I'll make you some breakfast, Pippa. You can't go without something inside you.' It was one of her mother's favourite sayings. It was just as if she, Pippa, were off for the day or to work.

They said goodbye in the porch, the

lights of the taxi showing through its window and the figure coming up the snow covered path.

'The motorway's open so there'll be no trouble getting to the airport,' the driver said. But Pippa wasn't listening. Sat hunched in a corner of the back seat shivering, her spirits as dark as the early dawn, and her mother's words echoing in her mind. 'You can always come home if things don't work out.'

During the flight Pippa's feeling of depression began to leave her. Saying goodbye to her mother and the lack of a definite date for the wedding had been mostly responsible, plus the unearthly hour of her departure. Things would have to work out — there would be no going back home. She loved Tomas.

Excitement began to mount in her as she sipped at a cup of coffee after breakfast. When the drinks trolley came around later, Pippa sitting on an inner seat next to the aisle, got into conversation with one of the steward-esses and could not resist telling her that she was on her way to Portugal to be married. The stewardess congratulated her, but refused the offer of a celebratory drink as they were not allowed on duty. How brave they were, Pippa thought, and how smart in their navy uniforms with the bowler type hat with its red band.

A few minutes later the stewardess came back smiling. 'The Captain's compliments — wishes you every happiness. You can have a drink on the airline.'

Pippa's spirits were beginning to soar. The brightness outside the windows, the effect of the drink she'd had already, the interested and occasionally envious glances from the stewardesses all contributed. Yes, she was lucky. Flying to the side of the man she loved.

By eleven-thirty she was outside the airport, in the warm, springlike air. Amongst the holidaymakers and the golf bags. The young women couriers standing by the line of coaches, passenger lists in their hands, and waiting to usher their charges aboard to be whisked away to their respective hotels. She had been one of those package holidaymakers last time. Now . . .

She stood wondering whether to go towards the line of parked cars visible some distance beyond the coaches, or wait where she was for a few minutes. Perhaps if she just had a look. Thought she would recognise his car. She was excited and just a little nervous, with a small but terrible inner voice questioning whether Tomas would be there or not.

14

Leaving her two cases she stepped between the coaches. A courier looked at her, pencil poised. Pippa shook her head and smiled, and suddenly felt alone in a strange country.

'Pippa.' The voice from behind her was unmistakable. She turned quickly. Tomas stood by her luggage amidst the receding tide of holiday makers. The white shirt collar out of the grey pullover accentuating his rugged dark handsomeness.

He had come as he had said he would. He was beautiful. Her eyes told him. Wonderful. Her heart was filled immediately.

'Pippa,' his voice was a sigh of longing. His eyes never left hers. He bent forward just as she was going to open her arms to him, grasped her by the shoulders and kissed her on the cheek. But his emotion showed through by the grip of his fingers against her flesh.

He picked up her luggage, headed away from the couriers and coaches and Pippa trotted alongside. 'Thought you might be waiting in the car,' she said breathlessly.

Tomas shook his head without looking at her. 'I saw the plane land, so many people.'

'Yes, they hold about three hundred,' she informed him.

It was the same car — the little Fiat. Tomas bundled the cases on to the back seat. Kept the door open for her. They got in. Then the wonderful sensation for Pippa of being crushed between his arms. She should have known his real welcome for her would be in the car — not in public. Moulded her body against his hungrily in the confines of the small car.

At last when he had let her go she gasped, 'Oh, Tomas, I had a terrible feeling that you might not be here.'

'And I thought the same, that I never see you again. That you would stay in England.' He smiled. 'You will see that I missed you.' His fingers caressed her bruised lips.

Pippa sighed against them. 'Me, too. You seemed a long way off, my love. I thought all the worst things.'

He looked down tenderly into her face. 'But now you feel better, eh?'

'Oh, yes, Tomas, now that we're together again.'

He searched her face, some concern on his own. 'You have become pale.' His mouth moved upwards at its corners. 'England has no Portuguese sun.'

Pippa smiled back wryly. 'It hasn't any sun at all at present. It was awful when I left.'

'You will be tired.'

'A little, I was up very early.'

'So was I.'

She stared up at him, realisation coming. 'You poor thing — fishing. You've been up all night and yet you've come to fetch me. That's very sweet of you, Tomas.' She pulled his dark head down, stroked it, their mouths meeting long and passionately.

Afterwards she said, 'Some day you may not have to fish every day. It's dangerous. Perhaps you can try something else.' She became aware of a strange look which appeared for an instant.

'Maybe.' He nodded. Then changed the subject. 'You have eaten on the plane?'

'Only a kind of late breakfast, but I can wait a while if you'd rather,' she assured him.

He eyed her seriously. 'One hour, we can eat at my house,' then smiled and added, 'your house now.'

'In that case I'll wait,' she exclaimed in excited anticipation.

Tomas released her and started the engine. Then he turned to her again. 'I forgot — I'm sorry. I do not ask about your mother. How is she?'

Pippa's hand flew to her breast. She

had meant to telephone her mother straight after the plane had landed. From the airport. She'd forgotten in the pleasure and excitement at seeing Tomas again. 'Good thing you reminded me, Tomas. She's well, thanks. Bit down in the dumps this morning — so was I. Promised I'd phone her from here. Do you mind?'

He shook his head. 'No, a mother is important person — she will be glad you safe.'

'Come with me, Tomas, please. You can speak to her as well.'

They got out and went back into the airport building. Pippa watched proudly as Tomas dialled the number from the paper she gave him. His strong brown fingers revolving the dial. The dark chest hairs straying over his open shirt collar.

She could hear the telephone ringing. Her mother would have been sat by it for the last hour. 'Hullo, Mum.' The excited yet anxious voice at the other end. 'Yes, I'm all right — of course I am. Good flight. Like spring here. Tomas met me.' The line was as clear as if her mother was a mile away. 'He's here now with me.' Pippa squeezed Tomas's hand. 'Yes, I'd something on the plane, and we're going to eat when we get to the house. Don't worry, I'm all right.' She heard that her aunt and uncle were coming later to spend the day with her mother. Was glad. It would be company for her.

Then Tomas spoke to Mrs. Gentle and Pippa smiled to herself. Tried to imagine her mother's expression. He promised her that he would look after Pippa and invited her to the wedding and hoped very much to see her. Before ringing off Pippa told her mother that she would call her again in a few days.

In the car afterwards and moving away from the airport, Pippa felt glad that Tomas had spoken to her mother. It served to bring the two families together immediately. She was also pleased that her aunt and uncle would be with her mother for the rest of the day. It would ease her loneliness for a while. Poor Mum. Pippa touched her eyes to halt the few tears.

Tomas glanced at her. 'You be all right, Pippa.' His hand touched her arm comfortingly.

She smiled at him. 'Tears of happiness, Tomas.'

He nodded understandingly. She was pleased that he had mentioned the wedding to her mother. It would give her something to think about and he had issued the invitation himself.

'It was sweet of you, Tomas, to invite her to the wedding. She'll be thrilled.'

Tomas looked momentarily at her. 'I think please the mother — please the daughter. I make good beginning.' His voice matched the provocative gleam in his eyes.

Pippa reached across. Kissed him on the cheek gratefully. Without taking his eyes off the road, he sought her hand and raised it to kiss its palm briefly.

Pippa, in a glow of happiness, watched the countryside go by. This was her country now. The white squat shuttered houses. Rows of orange trees. The umbrella pines. Villas for sale. New developments. The golf courses. The orange coloured buses towering over their small car.

They passed a donkey cart — an elderly couple in it, and a small short legged dog on a rope running desperately to keep up with the trotting donkey. Pippa turned in her seat, a sympathetic sound on her lips for the poor animal. Glanced at Tomas, guessed that he had noticed her reaction, a small mocking smile appearing at this obsession by the English for the comfort and well-being of the dog.

She remembered how when she had remarked one day to Tomas about the fact that the stray dogs did not appear ill-nourished, he had told her that that was because food waste was left lying about outside some hotels. Others tipped waste on to the rocks in some areas. That was why they did not starve. Also he had told her that to keep the numbers of stray dogs down, they took the oldest ones occasionally and put them to sleep humanely. So, Tomas had maintained, they did look after the dogs, but not in such a personal way.

Seeing a church reminded her that Tomas had not yet given a date for the wedding. But they could discuss it later. They now had all the time in the world. Her previous worry about it had diminished now that they were together again.

Pippa realised that she was becoming very hot and shrugged off the thick woollen cardigan she had worn underneath her coat when she had set off in the freezing cold that morning.

They drew up outside the house. The small square was tranquil, quiet. The sun was warm on her arms as she got out. The house looked brighter than when she had seen it before, the blue tiles sparkling as if they had been cleaned and the small openings in the white chimney edged in the same colour.

Tomas unlocked the door and stood aside for her to enter. The thought crossed Pippa's mind that he might have carried her across the threshold if they had been married. But perhaps they did not do that in Portugal. It seemed gloomy inside after the sunshine, her eyes taking their time to adjust. She saw a table with food ready upon it. A settee against a wall, and a tiny fireplace. An ancient looking stove in one corner and a flight of stairs against the far wall. At the side of the stairs there was another door.

Pippa turned back to Tomas. She wanted to fall into his arms. To be crushed in his love embrace. But Tomas was already stepping past her to the shutters. Pulling them back halfway, the light taking some of the sombreness of the room away.

Turning back to her he said in a strangely disinterested tone, 'Welcome to my house, Pippa.'

Pippa regarded him — a little hurt inside her. He had not said, their house, or your house as he had in the car earlier. Perhaps it was because they were not married yet. She moved further into the room noticing that the table was laid for two with what looked like a fish salad ready to serve. She also saw that a blanket was folded on the end of the settee. She glanced at Tomas to see an unfathomable expression. He nodded at the stairs. 'Your bedroom.'

She extended her hand to him. 'Aren't you coming with me?'

'No, I stay here. You will be hungry. I make it ready for you.'

Pippa climbed the stairs, puzzled and disappointed. The bedroom was sparsely furnished. A bed, a small dressing table, and a chair. She pulled at the inward opening doors and stepped on to the balcony, the sun yellowing the right hand side of it. The air felt warmer outside than in. Down below was Tomas's car. As she raised her eyes a curtain fluttered across the square. She smiled to herself — she would have to get used to that; it was only natural that they would be curious about a stranger — a foreigner in their midst.

She went up the short narrow curving stairway to the roof. It was private and peaceful behind the high parapet. She looked down again at the tiny square, and at the baked patch of ground at the rear of the house. It was barren. Would a child of hers ever play within its wooden fencing? Pippa turned and leaned her back against the parapet. Her eyes were caught by the church tower rising very close, it seemed, across the house tops. When was she going to come out of there a bride?

Downstairs again, Tomas smilingly handed her a cup of hot yellow liquid. 'I make you feel at home.'

Pippa gazed at him questioningly then sipped at the liquid, a tiny black thing floating on the top giving her a clue. It was tea of a kind. She sipped cautiously — it was awful. That was one thing she would have to teach him to make properly. Tomas was watching her reaction. She did not want to be churlish after he had tried to please her. 'It's kind of you, Tomas, and it's very nice, but I shall make it for you in future.' She smiled to herself. More for her satisfaction than his. It seemed that the only way that she would get a decent cup of tea was to make it herself.

They talked over the meal. Bream, sardines, mullet, rice, slivers of pota- toes, then a sweet of custard-like cake tasting of almonds. She looked at him shyly, in the confines of the small room. In a curious way it was like meeting him again for the first time.

That afternoon Tomas took her into the town. They walked and Pippa held on to his arm proudly, conscious of the envious glances given her by other women. Strangely though, her relation- ship with Tomas was easier outside that afternoon than it had been in the house. There had been some strain, a formality about their conversation over the meal. Several times she had caught him regarding her with a smouldering desire in his eyes. She had wanted desperately to return it and fulfil that desire, but if she submitted would he discard her afterwards? Perhaps she was being ultra cautious and unfair to him but the risk was there.

In the evening they dined out to celebrate her return to Portugal. They sat inside a huge barrel — one of several in the restaurant, the end cut away and the candlelight flickering on its rounded ceiling. It was a private and intimate little hideaway. Pippa was warm, flushed and in love with the man sitting opposite her.

That person put down his glass, leaned toward her, his arms on the table. 'I not go fishing tonight, Pippa,' he informed her. She stared at him, puzzled, and he smiled at this. 'You forget I have to work, but I stay at home with you tonight, meu bem. I see you all right first night, then you will not be lonely.' His dark eyes held a gleam heightened by the candlelight, and it turned Pippa's senses inside out.

It was true she had forgotten, and he was being considerate and thoughtful. A qualm of unease ran through her. To be alone most nights though, she had not given any thought to that.

Tomas must have guessed what had passed through her mind. Reaching across he parted her fingers with his own. 'I shall find other work so that I do not go out every night.' It was as if at that very moment he had settled something to his satisfaction. His tone was sure, confident, and it surprised her.

Pippa shook her head and smiled. 'No, it's your work, Tomas. I mustn't interfere. If the other wives can manage so can I.' She had been about to say 'women' but had persisted with wives. That's what she had come to Portugal for, to be a wife. Not just another woman.

Later they kissed passionately at every shadowy street corner on the way back. Pippa's emotions were torn, thwarted, her body tortured. In the house she showered, then dressed again, opened the door into the living room. Tomas was making his bed on the settee. 'Good night, Tomas.'

He turned and watched her ascend the stairs. 'Boa noite, Pippa, meu bem.' His voice was thick, low.

She shut the bedroom door noting that there was no lock upon it, and got into the lightly covered bed. The whole thing was stupid, she felt. She slept fitfully in her new home, once getting up to close the balcony doors, feeling the chill from the night air. Several times she heard Tomas moving about restlessly below. What an odd and strange situation she had got herself into, she reflected.

15

She must have dozed off again because the next thing she was aware of was Tomas standing just inside the bedroom door holding a cup. How long he had been there she could not guess. He was fully dressed. When he saw that she was awake he came to the bedside. 'I knock on the door, but you asleep.'

Pippa wondered. She was sure she would have heard him. It must have been a very light knock.

He handed her the cup. 'I make tea for you. I have to go out soon, Pippa.'

Raising herself she took it gratefully hoping that it would be an improvement on yesterday's. She glanced towards the balcony to see the sun already striking the houses opposite. Wouldn't be able to sit up bare armed in Halford at that time of the year.

'Thank you, Tomas. You're a dear. What time is it?'

'Oito.' He smiled down at her incomprehension. 'Eight. I try to teach you Portuguese now.'

'Oh.' It was too early for lessons. She took a sip, found that it was better than yesterday's. Knew that he was still gazing down at her. Where was he going so early in the morning?

She rested the cup on the small table at the bedside, reached out to squeeze his hand appreciatively. It was a mistake. His mouth came down on hers directly, his lips pressing hers apart avariciously. Forcing her head to the pillow, his body lying half upon her.

For a few moments she was caught up in the very fierceness of his desire, her body beginning to seek his. Felt the boring hardness of him through the covering sheets. His mouth moved away to her neck, her throat, like an animal gripping its prey. Then his lips drifted down to her breast tips under the nightdress. She gasped with her own

274

desire which threatened to engulf her. He was muttering in his own language.

Perhaps the fact of his lips leaving hers in some way freed the resistance in her. To fight the instincts of her body. Or maybe it was her native grit and stubbornness which finally reasserted itself. A word formed in her mind. Marriage! She had come out to Portugal for that. He should be fair to her.

She arched her body, squirmed to one side and slid off the bed. She staggered to the balcony doors, flung them open and faced him from there angrily. 'You promised marriage, Tomas, you promised. I want marriage. I love you, but I want marriage. The church is close enough. If you don't, tell me and I'll go back,' she shouted at him.

He got to his feet and faced her over the bed, his face loosened in his desire, eyes becoming slowly occupied again. His expression became set in his frustration. And Pippa felt as if she were facing a tiger about to spring.

Suddenly, and without saying a word, he turned swiftly and left her. She heard the outer door bang to, the car engine being started and revved, then the sound of it being driven away fiercely.

Pippa slumped on to the bed, stared miserably into space. She hadn't meant it to be like this. Angry words in her new home. The cup three quarters full still stood on the table by the bed. Tomas had been kind, thoughtful. Had brought her tea on her first morning. Perhaps he had meant to make love to her, the tea just an excuse to get into the bedroom. He was a red blooded male man. She couldn't really blame him. At that moment she hated herself. She washed then dressed despondently wondering where he had gone and how long it would be before he returned. He had said he had to go out before they had quarrelled.

Downstairs she made another cup of tea, drank it absent-mindedly, thinking that when he came back she would ask him outright about their wedding day. She smiled wryly, sadly — *if* he came back. Perhaps there was some problem holding up the wedding arrangements which he could not help, then in that case she would sleep with him. She wanted him as much as he wanted her. After all she was a modern girl. Others thought nothing of sleeping with their boy friends before marriage.

Pippa tried to busy herself about the house, dusting this, moving that, her eyes and ears alert for any sign of Tomas's return.

About twelve o'clock, the door opened. She turned swiftly from the table she was setting, contrite and joyful to welcome him home. 'Tomas, oh Tomas, I'm sorry . . . ' Her voice faded away in surprise and bitter disappointment. The girl Carmella stood just inside the door. Black haired, well groomed in a yellow dress with a grey light suede jacket. They stared at each other.

Then Pippa recovering somewhat said, 'What d'you want?' A sickening feeling was beginning to gnaw at her stomach.

The other's eyes flicked about the room insolently, then rested on Pippa again ignoring her question. 'Tomas, he leave you so soon?' Nodded to her own satisfaction. 'I tell you you not keep Tomas.' Wrinkled her nose. 'He not for you, for me yes.'

A rising anger took hold of Pippa at the woman Carmella's brazen rudeness and unannounced intrusion. 'Get out of my house,' she ordered dry-throated.

Carmella stood her ground. 'Your house?' She shook her head. 'Tomas's.' Gazed pityingly at Pippa. 'He have other house — much better.' Again satisfaction showed at poor Pippa's expression. 'You not know?'

'You're lying,' the latter flung back. Somehow she knew Carmella was not and the sinking feeling was growing worse. But Pippa clung on. Wasn't going to show any more hurt in front of

278

the other. 'We're going to get married,' she blurted out.

'Ah.' Carmella nodded knowingly. 'He tell you that, huh . . . ' She shrugged but her eyes had hardened and narrowed guardedly. 'When you get married?' she shot at Pippa.

'Sunday — next Sunday,' Pippa returned unthinkingly. She felt a triumph at Carmella's tightened lips and sudden uncertainty.

'Where?'

'The church up here. You're invited.' Pippa couldn't resist the latter remark. She wanted to hurt this woman.

'Not believe you.' Carmella half turned to the door then looked back viciously. 'I tell you where Tomas is. Down at boat with other woman.' She paused, savouring the sudden hurt on the other's face. Turned the knife. 'I see him at boat one hour ago.'

The door banged to after her and Pippa tottered to a chair, her thoughts floundering at the information given to her by Carmella. She tried to convince herself that none of it was true. She did not want to believe that Tomas was anything other than the man she knew and hoped to marry. Carmella was a jealous woman — would say anything to cause trouble and get Tomas for herself. And yet . . . Real doubts were now rising in Pippa's mind. Her Tomas. Was he after all just a shore-side philanderer, shallow and pleasure seeking? Butterflying to another woman so easily when denied?

Pippa laid her head in her arms on the table. The romantic dream was over. He'd never intended that house to be theirs together. She glanced around the room, made even more gloomy by her emotions. It was just a shell holding her shattered dream.

How long she remained there she did not know nor care, but then the hope and optimism submerged under the shock and despair began to reassert themselves again. Wasn't this just what that woman Carmella would want? To make trouble for them. To cast doubt between them. Tomas could be blameless. What sort of a wife-to-be was she if she believed everything that a jealous woman said?

A resolute determination took hold of her. She and Tomas had quarrelled. That was between themselves, nothing to do with anyone else. She would not believe anything Carmella had said until she found out for herself. Forced herself to think back over her confrontation with Carmella. Had she not said that Tomas was down at the boat? Did she mean his sailing boat? A shiver ran through Pippa. She prayed that he would be alone on it.

The sun was sinking as she left the house hurriedly, and unmindful of the curious glances at her obvious distress as she passed people and dodged by inches the cars and the occasional bus in her efforts to reach the boat and Tomas, and put her tortured mind at rest. Painful as it was for her, she forced herself to reason as to the whereabouts of Tomas. Which boat? The answer was all too easy. His sailing boat had a cabin on it, the fishing one did not — not a proper one anyway. There was no doubt he would take another woman to the cabined boat.

Memories came as she turned into the main street and headed for Fisherman's beach. She saw the chestnut seller. She and Tomas had shared some. The outdoor café and bar where they had sat content together over a drink. Suddenly she felt desperately lonely, lost in her new country.

By the sea wall was parked a small car. Pippa's eyes fastened on it. Tomas's car. She did not know its number but she was certain it was his. Drawing a deep breath she struck out across the beach oblivious of the few people walking the edge of the sea and the fishermen between the boats. Her eyes searched the water, half wishing that she would not see the boat and afraid of what she may find upon it.

She made for the next stretch of beach remembering that that was where he had taken her the day they had sailed together. What a wonderful day that had been! A romantic dream had been hers for a while in a hard and cynical world.

She recognised Tomas before the boat. The latter further inshore than it had been when she had seen it the last time. He was by the cabin door seemingly about to enter. Pippa shouted his name. The evening was still and her voice carried. She saw him turn, look shorewards. She waved and hailed him again.

Fear struck at her heart as he appeared to close the cabin door hurriedly before turning again in her direction. His manner and posture was one of indecision.

'I want to come aboard,' she called, seeing the dinghy at the boat's side.

He gave a peremptory wave of his hand then clambered over the side into it, covering something in the bottom before he sat down and picked up the oars.

A few minutes later the dinghy grounded and he waded through the shallow water towards her, his trousers rolled to his calves. 'You should not come by yourself — a woman alone,' he said.

'It isn't dark yet, plenty of people about,' she replied stiffly, thinking that any danger there was — a threat to their relationship — would be in the boat.

He stopped in front of her, did not attempt to touch her. Stared at her from under the peak of his cap with a questioning impatience.

'I had to see you.'

'I come home soon, nearly finished. Go back to the car, Pippa. Wait for me,' he ordered.

'No, Tomas, I'd rather stay here. What have you been doing on the boat?'

He avoided her gaze, glanced behind him. 'I look after it, some things to do,' he replied vaguely.

Suspicion already in her heart was

growing fast. 'Are you going back to it now?'

He nodded away from her.

'Let me come with you, Tomas.'

'I not be long. You wait in the car, better you do that.' There was a trace of anxiety and irritability in his tone.

'Please, Tomas, take me to the boat. It means a lot to me.'

He turned set-faced, regarded her a moment. 'All right,' and set off to the water.

Pippa stared at his back, surprised at his sudden acquiescence to her plea. Then taking off her shoes she followed him.

In the dinghy her eyes fell on the bulge under the tarpaulin in the bow. There was a silence on the way across broken only by the splash of the oars. So different, thought Pippa miserably, from the times before. Then it had been animated talk and looks, the excitement of love. Now just an awkward and strained unease between them.

She watched Tomas make the dinghy

fast, then pick up the tarpaulin and whatever was underneath and hump it aboard. Following, she was surprised to be offered an unexpected hand over the side. She thanked him abruptly and sat in the stern. Had that hand been caressing another woman recently?

It was cool in the boat's cockpit and she remembered vividly the last time she had been there. Then he had asked her to marry him. Since that day the boat had had a special place in her heart.

Tomas stood with his back to the cabin door eyeing her questioningly. 'I bring you — you are here. Now . . .' he said shortly with a half shrug.

Pippa looked up at him. 'I — I want to see inside,' she said unsteadily.

'It is locked.'

'Please unlock it, Tomas. It's so important to me.'

'Why? What d'you want to see?'

It was what she did not wish to see. 'I've got to — I must.' Her voice was thin, nerves giving way.

'No.' He shook his head. 'I cannot.' There was a tenseness in his regard of her.

'Why? Why not, Tomas?' she cried hoarsely, her soul bared on her face. 'You have a woman in there, I know.' Pippa was horrified at what she was saying. It must be someone else speaking the words.

'A woman!' Anger gleamed in his eyes, but his voice was level as he replied, 'You do us both an injustice, Pippa. I know I was hasty and selfish this morning. But now you accuse me — say I have a woman. You are hasty now.' His words came quicker. 'You think I want other woman when I ask you to marry me and bring you from England?' He banged the cabin top with his fist, ejaculated some word in his languge. Then he plunged his hand into his pocket, brought out a key and thrust it into the cabin lock. Tore open the door savagely. 'Now,' he flung at her, 'find the woman.'

With a terrible feeling Pippa stepped

into the gloom of the cabin. Boxes lay piled on the floor — cardboard boxes.

'Go on,' commanded Tomas harshly from behind her, 'open them.'

Pippa took hold of the lid of one nearest, pulled it open. Bottles — full ones.

'Take them out. Look at them,' Tomas ordered sharply.

Wretchedly Pippa took some out. Whisky! Rum! Gin!

Suddenly, Tomas was tearing the other lids apart. 'You see drink! Not woman. Drink! Now you know.'

Dumbfounded Pippa sank on to the bunk. She didn't understand. Buried her head in her hands dimly conscious of Tomas leaving the cabin.

16

Some time later, she couldn't have told how long, Tomas re-entered. Pippa felt his weight lower the mattress beside her. She felt her hands being grasped in his.

'Please listen to me, Pippa, then you will understand,' he said in kinder, gentler tones.

She looked up slowly at him, saw that the anger and the tension had gone from him. The dark eyes held only a relieved resignation. 'Oh, Tomas, I'm sorry,' she sighed.

He shook his head slightly. 'No, you have made it so that I have no need to go on lying to myself.' She gazed at him incomprehendingly as he went on, 'You know me as Tomas the fisherman. We met on the beach. I was the fisherman, yes?'

Her eyes clung to his as she nodded.

'But I was not always the fisherman, Pippa. Only for three years. You see, my father was head of a large wine producing company. I was the eldest son. I went to a good college.' A little smile appeared. 'My English as you know can be better at times. Then when I left I went into the family business. I did well, money, a big car, this boat, the use of the family villa. I lacked for nothing except . . .'

He paused in reflection for a moment then continued, 'But one day I thought to myself that I had not made that business, I had just stepped into my father's place. He had done all the work. He had made the business what it was, and I felt that I had done nothing.' He shrugged. 'Oh, I did my best, he was pleased, but somehow I felt that I needed to build something of my own — to make my own way. Do you understand?'

Pippa was beginning to. She freed her hand and stroked the side of his face tenderly, but he grasped it again as if the better to concentrate on his story and went on, 'I left the business, he did not understand. Thought I was mad. So I became a fisherman. The sea is in my family's blood a generation or two back.' He sighed, some of the tension returning to his features. 'After the good money and living, the earnings from fishing seemed very poor. This year I was beginning to feel desperate. I did not wish to go back and tell my father that I had failed on my own, and yet I was not satisfied at the money I was making. I had kept this boat intending to sell it, but,' his shoulders lifted again, 'I could not — it was the only thing that separated me from the other fishermen. It was something of value.' His grip tightened on Pippa. 'Then I saw you.' A look of shame appeared as he paused then carried on, 'Nothing else mattered. I fell in love with you, was frightened I would lose you, you know the rest — I nearly lost you. I was a fool.' Tomas half turned away, grimacing in sudden anger at himself.

Understanding and love shone in Pippa's face. 'Oh, Tomas, if only I'd known! I would not have cared what sort of work you did.'

His dark eyes bored into hers with longing. 'I wanted to marry you, but could not support you properly on the money I earned from fishing.'

Pippa sighed. 'You should have told me, I would have found work.'

'No,' he ejaculated fiercely, startling her. His features had become proud, commanding. 'No, my wife would not work. Not a wife of Tomas da Silva.' His face softened somewhat though a frown remained. 'I worried that if you returned to England you would not come back to me, so I asked you to marry me though I did not know how I was going to support you.' He smiled wryly. 'I did not catch much fish when you were away. I think too much about us.'

If Pippa could have freed her hands from his she would have been unable to refrain from locking her arms about him. A rising joy was beginning to overcome her. This wonderful man by her side was already wiping away the miserable memory of the earlier part of the day.

Tomas was speaking again. 'Then I think of a new idea to make money so that I could marry you quickly.' He nodded at the boxes. 'I would sail to Morocco with that — I should be paid well.'

Pippa stared at him in concerned astonishment. 'You mean smuggle the stuff in?'

'Yes,' he nodded, but — '

'No! No, Tomas,' she interrupted, fear for him giving her strength to break her hands free from his. Grasped his arms. 'You mustn't — it's dangerous. We can — '

'Don't worry,' broke in Tomas, 'I shall not,' he assured her. 'I know it was wrong now.'

'You don't have to risk your life or go to prison for me, Tomas. I'll make do and we'll manage, just you see.'

He smiled more freely than he had done for some time. 'I have made up my mind. You are too important to me, more important than my independence. I have decided to go back into the business if they will have me.'

'Of course they will, Tomas. You obviously helped to continue the success of the business when you were part of it,' Pippa went on reassuringly. 'After all you must have brought your own individual ideas to it. I'm sure you have different ones from your father. An individual can still enjoy some independence in a family business like yours,' she finished earnestly. Truth to tell she was only just beginning to realise the implications for her.

The stern set of Tomas's features was beginning to soften. He looked like a man whose worries were relinquishing their grip and slipping away one by one. He gazed at her in admiration and love. 'You have fire, Pippa. Your eyes, they flash like lightning from a blue sky.'

Fear for him still showed as she replied, gazing into his face intently, 'Tomas da Silva, never mind my eyes. Promise me faithfully that you will get rid of this stuff.' She waved her hands at the boxes. 'And never think of doing that again. I'll marry you poor rather than have you in prison or at the bottom of the sea.'

'I promise, Pippa,' he agreed. 'I decided when you came aboard.'

'Oh, thank God, my love,' she breathed in huge relief.

Tomas moved closer, looking puzzled. Put an arm around her shoulder. 'How did you know to find me here?'

A shadow crossed Pippa's face at the traumatic memory of a few hours ago. 'That woman Carmella called this morning. She — '

'Carmella?' Tomas exclaimed. He drew his face away to look directly into Pippa's. 'What did she say?' he grated, his voice low with a suppressed anger.

'Oh, it doesn't matter now, Tomas.

Things have changed, I realise.'

'Perhaps, but I must know, Pippa.' His tone brooked no argument.

Pippa sighed. 'Oh, well she said you had another woman here on the boat, and . . . ' She saw the taughtened muscles in his neck. 'And that you had another house and that it was going to be for someone else.' Pippa shook her head helplessly. 'I've forgotten exactly what she said. I don't want to remember now. I was very sad.'

Tomas's eyes encompassed her face in great compassion and tenderness. 'And I leave you alone this morning to that,' he exploded in self-recrimination, then uttered something fiercely in his own language. 'You don't understand Portuguese. It is just as well,' he said harshly. He gazed around him, seemingly helpless in his anger. Then he turned to her quelling it with an obvious effort. 'One thing, Pippa, meu bem you lack is conceit.' He nodded, managing a smile at her surprise. 'You are so beautiful. I love you. Did you

296

think that I would go with another woman? I knew her once, she thought she owned me. She's nothing.'

For Pippa the pendulum of happiness and misery had nearly reached its full sweep. Just one thing remained. She placed her finger tips inside the open front of Tomas's shirt. Twisted the hairs between them. Her voice held a note of apprehension. 'Tomas, my love. I hope you don't mind, I couldn't help it — I was so miserable, but that woman, she seemed to know everything. Didn't believe that we were going to marry. I — I told her we were going to be married on Sunday. I couldn't help it, Tomas, I just said it.' She raised her eyes slowly not knowing what expression she would see on his face. To her utter amazement she saw absolute wonderment.

'How — how did you know?' he stammered.

'W — what d'you mean, Tomas?'

'That we are going to be married on Sunday. I told no one.'

'We're going to be married on Sunday?' Pippa's voice was a hoarse, incredulous, excited sound.

'Yes, I was going to tell you tonight. I went straight to the church when I left you this morning to arrange it.'

Pippa was dizzy on a roundabout of ecstasy. 'I just said it on the spur of the moment. It was something I'd prayed for. I thought you'd forgotten, or did not want me any more.'

Both of Tomas's arms tightened around her. His vitality and virility surging against her body. 'I think,' he uttered huskily, 'that I was a very successful fisherman.' A glint of humour shone through his desiring eyes. 'I caught you. I shall be the envy of every fisherman in Portugal.'

Their lips touched, held fiercely. Then Pippa wrenched hers away with an effort. 'Close the door,' she whispered. The pendulum had touched and stopped.

★ ★ ★

Pippa, on Tomas's arm, emerged from the cool interior of the church into the sunshine to be surrounded by smiling, happy people — people she had not known until a few days ago. It had been a hectic time with visits from Tomas's parents, his two brothers, and his sister Maria who had quickly struck up a friendship with Pippa, and had helped her prepare and dress for the important day. It was a whole new world and family, she thought, as she gazed joyously on the congratulating faces.

Love for Tomas making her radiant she stood in the black wedding dress that she had promised she would wear. It had been important to him, she knew, the dress having been handed down from generation to generation. The sombre look of the dress was relieved by the silver lace work of a large heart enclosing a key on its front. She fingered the end of the white lace shawl over her shoulders — a special present from Tomas. Interwoven in the centre of it were the words 'Sempre *noivos*'. He had told her it meant always together.

The church bell rang out and above its sound Tomas said something to her and pointed beyond a group of guests. A woman was stepping out of a silver coloured limousine which had just drawn up in front of the church.

A man moved forward — Tomas's father, hiding the woman's face for a moment. They shook hands, Senor Da Silva bowing and then turning to lead the woman towards the bridal pair.

Pippa stared astounded. Her mother. It was a vision, it must be. Her mother here! She heard Tomas's voice in her ear.

'I did my best. Unfortunately there wasn't a plane that would get her here in time for the ceremony.'

Joy upon joy. A few tears as they embraced. Mother's and daughter's faces telling all to the other. There would be time to talk at the reception.

How smart her mother looked in blue, and well, and how wonderfully handsome Tomas looked as Pippa introduced them to each other. Saw the approval on both faces and was glad.

'What a lovely wedding present, Tomas,' she said looking up at him adoringly. 'I can't believe it.'

'I telephoned her. I made a note of the number when you phoned her at the airport. I persuaded her to come. She's staying for two weeks as my family's guest at Portimoa.'

'Oh, Tomas, how marvellous! I can't get over it — so kind and thoughtful of you.'

Then Tomas led Pippa to another car, leaving Mrs. Gentle to be gathered into the midst of the family who were to follow. They passed the end of the street where the house was situated.

Pippa looked at Tomas in surprise. 'I thought the reception was going to be at the house.'

'It is, meu bem,' said Tomas with a mysterious smile.

'But . . . ' Pippa sighed in happiness. Gave up trying to understand. She was sat in the back of a wedding car holding the hand of her husband. That was all that mattered.

A few minutes later she realised that they were on the road to Monte Sirocco village. Then they were at the cross roads, and up the road she glimpsed the hotel where she had stayed. Another mile further on the car swung into a drive fringed with bushes, flowers, and pine trees. The drive widened, running alongside a green lawn on which a water sprinkler played. The car stopped at the steps of a long low villa, set on terracing. Huge curved windows lay beyond a railed terrace, and a wide stairway curved to the roof. The villa was dazzling white and expensive looking against the background of blue sky.

Tomas got out, looked back in at her, smiling. 'This is where the reception is taking place. Here, at your house — the villa Praia-da-Oura.'

Pippa clung to his arm. 'My house!' she uttered weakly.

'Yes, it is a wedding present from the family to us. It used to be our holiday villa — away from the business. The other house,' he added pointedly. He indicated the car they had just arrived in, which was being parked. 'And that is your car.'

Pippa gazed across the green sheltered lawn at it. White, opulent and gleaming. The whole thing was a beautiful dream — it couldn't be anything else. Yet, Tomas's hand through her arm was real and firm enough. He began to lead her to the door of the villa which was edged in light blue matching the chimney above.

Pippa saw an elderly couple standing to one side of it awaiting them. 'Isabella and Jose, they have been with the family as long as I can remember,' explained Tomas. 'They wanted to welcome you.' He halted, looked at her, desire and love bared on his face. 'You loved me when I was poor. Now will you love me when I am rich?'

As she gazed at him, Pippa knew that

mere words could never convey all she felt for him. Suddenly a car horn sounded in the drive behind them. The guests had begun to catch up.

Much, much later after the reception, when everyone had gone, Tomas picked Pippa up in his arms. Carried her to the bedroom, laid her gently upon the bed, her head sinking luxuriously into the soft pillow. His expression one of passion soon to be unleashed.

He leaned over her, whispered deeply, 'I remember when I put a rose on your pillow. Then you hated me. Now another rose lies on the pillow. Does she love me?'

And Senhora Pippa da Silva's answer was to bring her husband's lips down to meet hers.

THE END